COMPANIONS
of the NIGHT

Other books by Vivian Vande Velde

USER UNFRIENDLY

DRAGON'S BAIT

A HIDDEN MAGIC

A WELL-TIMED ENCHANTMENT

ONCE UPON A TEST:
Three Light Tales of Love

COMPANIONS
of the NIGHT
VIVIAN VANDE VELDE

Jane Yolen Books

Harcourt Brace & Company

San Diego   New York   London

Library of Congress Cataloging-in-Publication Data
Vande Velde, Vivian.
Companions of the night/Vivian Vande Velde.—1st ed.
p. cm.
"Jane Yolen books."
Summary: When sixteen-year-old Kerry Nowicki helps a young man escape from a group of men who claim he is a vampire, she finds herself faced with some bizarre and dangerous choices.
ISBN 0-15-200221-9
[1. Vampires—Fiction.] I. Title.
PZ7.V2773Co 1995
[Fic]—dc20 94-30106

Designed by Trina Stahl
First edition A B C D E

Printed in the United States of America

Dedicated with love to

Allan and Barbara

Gretchen and Bruce

Herb and Donna

Oh, my love, my darling,

I've hungered

for your touch

a long, lonely time.

Time goes by

so slowly

and time

can do so much. . . .

—"Unchained Melody"

(A. North / H. Zaret)

COMPANIONS
of the NIGHT

CHAPTER ONE

WHEN IAN CAME into Kerry's room to ask for a favor, it never occurred to her that her four-year-old brother could ask her to do something that might get her killed.

"What kind of favor?" she asked, sticking a finger in her book to keep her place. It was almost eleven o'clock at night, her second period literature teacher had promised a test tomorrow, and she still had fifty pages to go, with the author seeming in no hurry to wrap things up.

"I left Footy at the laundry," Ian said. Footy was Ian's stuffed koala bear.

"Ian," Kerry pointed out—the same thing she'd pointed out the instant he'd entered her room—"it's the middle of the night. You're supposed to be asleep in bed, I'm supposed to be asleep in bed, Dad *is* asleep. . . ."

Ian's bottom lip began to tremble, and Kerry rested her forehead in her hand.

"Don't cry," she said. Ever since Mom had left, Kerry couldn't take it when Ian cried. "Maybe you forgot him at Greg's"—Ian started shaking his head—"or in Daddy's car?"

"No," Ian said. "I was playing under the counter where you fold your stuff. You know the pink stripy one that doesn't match the others?"

Kerry didn't know, but she nodded to keep him going.

"I was using the laundry cart as a fort. I know that's where I left him, under the pink stripy counter. Can't you go and get him?"

Kerry shook her head. "I've only got a learner's permit, so I'm not allowed to drive unless there's somebody who has a license with me," she explained. "I'd get in trouble with Dad *and* the police. Footy will be fine one night without you. It'll be like a campout for him."

If Ian had thrown a tantrum, he would have been easier to resist. But he stood there silently, tears running down his face. Then, very quietly, he said, "It won't be like a campout. Somebody will steal him."

"Ian, munchkin, the kind of people who go to laundries in the middle of the night are not the kind of people who steal ragged little koala bears."

"Footy's not ragged," Ian said. "And if it was Corny, you wouldn't leave *her*."

Kerry looked to her dresser at the unicorn she'd had since she was two. Now that Kerry was sixteen, Corny rarely traveled farther than from the bed to the dresser, but Ian had made his point. "All right, all right." Kerry took her finger out of the book. "But you stand by Daddy's door and make sure you hear him snoring, or I'm not moving. And if Dad wakes up, tell him . . ." *Tell him* what? *What story would he possibly believe? And what am I doing coaching a four-year-old to lie? Hadn't there been enough lies in this family in the year before Mom moved out?* "Tell him I'll be back soon," she finished.

She shooed Ian out of the room and pulled her jeans on, tucking in her IF IT'S MORNING DON'T TALK TO ME night-shirt. She'd be wearing her jacket, and anyway, she thought, if anybody stopped her, she was going to be in too much trouble to be embarrassed by what she was wearing. She pulled her hair back into a ponytail without even checking in a mirror.

This was all her mother's fault. They wouldn't even have to go to the laundry if her mother hadn't abandoned them, moving from Brockport, New York, to Somewhere-or-other, Florida, to study to be a private investigator—and only one postcard since. She had left the car because the man she went with had a better one, but she'd taken the washer and dryer.

What kind of mother leaves her family, letting her kids run the risk of losing their koala bears in laundries? Kerry asked herself. It was a dangerous question, because the answer was easy: *a mother who doesn't like her kids.*

Still, once Kerry had tiptoed out of the house—and not counting the fear of getting stopped by the police—it seemed such a simple, safe little task.

FIVE MINUTES LATER, Kerry pulled up in front of the Quick-Clean Laundry. The street was dark but not deserted. Next door the Strand Theatre was all lit up. The movie must have just ended because there were people still coming out. Down the other way was a pizza place where the college kids hung out. She could smell the tomato sauce and hear the music.

The laundry, of course, was always open. In a college town where half the kids lived off campus, there had to be a twenty-four-hour laundry.

Her dad hadn't taught her parallel parking yet, and Kerry ended up a good three feet from the curb and overlapping two parking places. That left half a space behind her car before the corner, and a parking space and a half before the last of the cars from the movie crowd, but she told herself she was only going to be here a sec and didn't need to worry about getting ticketed.

As she opened the door, she was greeted by the smell of warm wet soap. All the lights were on—she'd seen that from the street because the place was half windows—but nobody was there. Not even the little guy who ran the place, the one who made change and sold overpriced single-wash boxes of soap and fabric softener if you forgot to bring some from home, and yelled if he caught you leaving without cleaning out the lint tray. Kerry had known that the little guy couldn't be there all twenty-four hours that the place was open, but she was amazed there wasn't *somebody* around to make sure people didn't come in and pry open the money boxes. She felt creepy being there all alone so late at night.

Grab Footy, she thought, *and then get home.* Fighting a yawn, she realized she was way too tired to tackle her literature project. She'd just have to bluff her way through the test.

She glanced around the shop and immediately identified the counter Ian had been talking about. The counters were all white with gold speckles except that one, last remnant of a previous decor or an addition from somebody's leftover something-or-other. She thought, *Well, that was easy.*

Except, of course, Footy wasn't there.

4

"Stupid bear," she muttered.

She crawled under the counter just to make sure. There was a paper pamphlet—probably one of the owner's Bible tracts that he was always trying to pass out—and maybe Footy could be hidden behind it. The floor was gritty with spilled soap that stuck to the palms of her hands and, when she tried to wipe her hands clean, stung where she'd bitten the skin near her nails. She poked at the paper, wondering what the chances were of mice lurking around a place like this.

No Footy, but at least no mice either. Only a razor blade, which someone had probably brought to open the boxes of detergent.

Idiot! Kerry thought at whoever had dropped it, remembering how Ian had been crawling under here. Carefully she picked the blade up and backed out from underneath the counter.

Her good deed paid off, for it wasn't until she put the razor down in the ashtray on the desk with the cash register that she noticed Footy sitting on top of the pile of religious pamphlets.

"You, mister," she said, picking up the bear and shaking a finger at him. Then she dropped her voice to a whisper because the only other sound was the hum of the fluorescent lights. "You are in deep trouble, and you're grounded until you're thirty-seven. Whatever that works out to in bear years."

She hadn't even lowered her finger when the back door burst open.

The owner, Kerry thought as she whirled around to face whoever it was that was making such a commotion coming in. *Mr. Quick-Clean.* He must have stepped out to get a cup of coffee or a slice of pizza and then realized how long he'd left his place unattended.

As she turned, Footy smacked against the cash register and slipped from her fingers to the floor. Instinctively Kerry bent down to pick him up, knowing, even as she shifted her balance, that this was the last thing she should do. She should call out "Hello," step forward, let the owner see that she was here, look like a paying customer—or at least like someone who had a legitimate reason to be here and not like someone trying to hide or to break into the cash register.

But before she could straighten, she saw the people coming in through the door: four men, three of them dragging one who was—Kerry felt her heart stop, then start again at a frenzied pace—gagged and bloodied, with his hands tied behind his back.

Kerry dropped to her hands and knees under the desk.

A drug deal gone bad, she thought. *Or a gang fight.* Not that there was much of that sort of thing in Brockport, but she'd seen enough cop shows to guess.

And she was caught right in the middle of it.

One of the men kicked the prisoner behind the leg so that he dropped to his knees and his face was momentarily on a level with Kerry's. Young, she saw, and scared, which was natural enough. It took a second for his eyes to focus on her, and then one of the other men jerked him backward by the hair so that his back was to one of the stainless steel laundry tubs. They began tying his already bound hands to the thick steel leg of the tub.

Then the one who was doing the tying looked up and saw her. "What the hell—," he started.

And in that moment, which Kerry recognized was probably her last chance to get to her feet and run to the front door screaming for help, she was too scared to move.

The prisoner tried to break away while their attention

was diverted, but the man in front knocked him back so that his head cracked against the side of the tub. The third man reached over and grabbed hold of Kerry's arm while the one with the rope returned to tying.

Still holding on to Footy, Kerry was dragged out from beneath the desk and hauled to her feet.

"She one of them?" one of the men asked. "Or just a thief?"

"No," she whispered, unable to take her gaze off the young man, who looked on the verge of passing out. They were going to kill him. And then they were going to kill her for seeing them kill him. "I— I— I—"

"Get the blinds down, you idiot," the other man said. "Do you want anyone passing down Main Street to see what's going on?"

"I—," Kerry said as, behind her, she heard the blinds crash down, one after the other, then the doors being locked, both front and back. "I—"

The one holding her pulled her in for a closer look. He was a black man, the only one of the group who was. He was also about twice the size of anybody else there. Taller. Broader. Kerry's arm, even padded by her jacket, was lost in the massiveness of his hand. "She's just a kid," the big guy said, which sounded encouraging, except for the fact that he was practically breaking her arm.

Kerry nodded emphatically.

"This other one's barely more than a kid. They make 'em when they're still kids?"

Nobody said anything, and Kerry wasn't sure what was the right answer. She didn't even understand the question. *No,* she suspected. Under the circumstances, *no* to everything except the suggestion that they send her home.

Before she could get her voice working again, one of the

other two grabbed a handful of hair, and her head was forced around to face him. "I didn't do anything," she managed, which seemed an even safer answer. "Please don't hurt me."

The black man, still holding her arm, used his free hand to feel over her arm.

Kerry felt her knees start to buckle. *Better to be passed out for this anyway,* she thought.

But the man was moving down her arm, which was an unexpected direction, to her hand, which he jiggled as though to see how well it was attached. Then he crunched her fingers together; but when she winced, he stopped. "I don't think she's one of them," he said.

"I don't think I'm one of them either," Kerry agreed.

"Shut up," said the man who was still holding her hair.

"Why are you here?" the third man asked, the one who'd been in charge of tying their prisoner.

And it was only when Kerry shifted her gaze to him that she recognized him: the little guy who ran the place. Mr. Quick-Clean himself, who sat there all day reading the Bible and trying to get people to read his religious pamphlets.

"Why are you here?" he repeated, sounding even more menacing than before.

"I'm sorry," she whispered. "I just came to get my little brother's bear." She tried to indicate Footy, but he was in the hand whose arm was being slowly pulled out of its socket.

Footy dropped and landed with a soft plop.

"You've seen me here before," she continued. *What's he doing?* she thought all the while. *Drug dealers and gang members don't encourage people to read the Bible.* "You know me," she insisted. "My name is Kerry Nowicki. I come here with my father, Stephen, and my brother, Ian. My father always buys a helium balloon at the Lift Bridge Book Shop before we come here, and he ties it to Ian's wrist so that we don't lose track of him because he's shorter than the machines." She couldn't tell from the man's face whether he recognized her or not. "We were in this evening after dinner. Ian forgot his bear under the counter near the door. But you must have found him, or somebody did, because when I came in, he was up here by the cash register."

The man looked from her to the bear. Finally, *finally*, he nodded. "Yeah." He nodded again. He told the others, "They come in once or twice a week."

"Always after dinner?" asked the one with his hand still in her hair.

Whatever the significance of that question, the laundry owner looked straight into his eyes. "No. Saturdays, too, sometimes. Saturdays, it's mornings or afternoons."

The one loosened his grip on her arm, still holding on though she no longer had to stand on tiptoe; and the other let go of her hair entirely. That one said, "Bad timing now, though."

You can say that again, Kerry thought.

Instead, he said, "She could've become one of them since last Saturday."

Kerry's heart sank at the look this possibility brought to the owner's face.

"Maybe," he said.

"One way or the other," said the one who still had her arm, "we can't let her go, not till this is over."

"This" had to be their prisoner. "This" probably meant killing him. She saw that he hadn't lost consciousness after all. She was tempted to promise that if they let her go she wouldn't go to the police, she wouldn't tell anybody what she'd seen. But she couldn't do that with him looking right at her. And they wouldn't believe her anyway.

"Don't be afraid," the owner told her. "Not if you're what you say you are."

What? Kerry wanted to scream at him. *I haven't SAID I'm anything. What do you THINK I am?* But it was probably best not to say anything that might be construed as argument.

The owner said, "Nobody wants to hurt you."

She had serious doubts about that, but she forced herself to nod.

"We're just going to keep you here till morning. Then we'll bring you home ourselves."

"What are you going to do to me between now and morning?" she asked, her voice quavering uncontrollably.

"Nothing," the owner assured her. "Sit here quietly and don't give us any trouble, and we won't even have to tie you up."

Her voice got even more quavery as she looked at their prisoner. "What are you going to do to *him?*"

The one who'd been pulling her hair answered, "That's none of your damn business."

The owner gave him a be-quiet look. To Kerry, he said, "If he behaves himself, we won't lay a finger on him either."

"We won't need to," the hair puller said.

"Let her go, Roth," the owner said to the man still holding her arm.

And slowly, as though ready to grab again if she even thought of trying to escape, the big black man, Roth, loosened his grip.

"See," the owner said. "We can be calm and reasonable. Sit down"—she sat immediately, on the floor, right where she'd been standing—"don't talk, don't interfere. There's more to this than you could ever understand."

Kerry nodded. She was sitting facing the young man. There was a ghastly smear of blood on the floor where they had dragged him backward, indicating an injury to his leg, though she couldn't see anything because he had his legs under him, which had to hurt. And there was more blood running down the side of his face from a cut she could, thankfully, barely glimpse under his dark hair. His eyes were blue—she'd noticed that when he'd first looked at her. Dark hair, blue eyes, fair skin. His coloring emphasized the redness of the blood that had spattered his white SUNY Brockport sweatshirt. Of course, the shirt wasn't proof that he actually went to the college.

But he looked like he might. Probably a freshman—she guessed he wasn't that much older than she, maybe nineteen, which would put him at about half the age of the two men Kerry had never seen before: Roth, who looked like a football player, and the hair puller, who had the football jacket. NEW YORK GIANTS, it read. The laundry owner had to be in his fifties.

And none of them—*none* of them—fit Kerry's picture of gang members or drug lords or international terrorists.

The owner went to the pay phone on the wall behind the desk, where he dialed a number without having to look it up. Whoever he was calling must have been asleep or away from the phone, for it took the interval of several rings before he said, "Marcia? . . . Yeah. We've got one of them. . . . At the laundry. Ken's dead. I'll explain later. . . . Marcia, there's no time for that now. Come around the back—the doors're locked." There was a longer pause, during which Kerry thought she was going to faint from fear: somebody was dead already. Then the owner sighed. "Of all the . . . Well, hurry up about it. . . . Yeah, I know." He hung up.

"What now?" the man named Roth asked.

"She needs to stop for batteries for the video camera."

"Dimwit." Roth said it with resigned lack of enthusiasm, as though they were used to this Marcia—whoever she was—being a dimwit.

On the other hand, judging by the look the laundry owner gave Roth, maybe Marcia was Mrs. Quick-Clean.

"I think," said the New York Giants fan, "we don't need the camera to get started."

Everybody turned to look at the prisoner.

Kerry thought he was holding up a lot better than she would have. His eyes, above the gag, looked scared but defiant. She would have been crying and trying to let them know that she was willing to do or say whatever it was they wanted of her. Of course, she thought, that was easier for her to think, since she didn't know *what* they wanted of him.

"Take the gag off," Roth said.

"He isn't going to cooperate," New York Giants said. Despite what they'd said earlier, he sounded like he was looking forward to the prisoner not cooperating.

"I think we should wait for Marcia," the owner suggested. "Maybe closer to dawn he'll be more reasonable."

New York Giants took the gag off anyway.

He's waiting for him to say something, Kerry thought, *something like "butthead" or "asshole," and then he's going to beat the hell out of him.*

But the young prisoner didn't lash out at his captors. He spoke, all in a rush, to Kerry: "My name's Ethan Bryne. When you get out of this, tell the police—"

12

New York Giants kicked him, hard, in the stomach.

He doubled over, gasping for breath.

"Don't give her any of that bull," New York Giants said. "You don't want the police in this any more than we do. Less, even."

"Tell them—"

He kicked the boy again, this time in the ribs, since he couldn't get to the stomach. Then he drove his elbow into the kid's back, between his shoulders.

Kerry put her arms up over her head to avoid seeing. And for protection. "Stop it or I'll scream!" Though she recognized the safest course was not to get involved, Kerry was screaming already—or as close to it as she could get, with her throat constricted by terror. *"Stop it, stop it, stop—"*

She was expecting that they would kick her, too, and she was expecting it to be in the face, because she'd just finished with her retainers after two and a half years of braces, and getting her teeth broken was close to the worst thing she could imagine after all that.

But Roth was yelling at New York Giants, "Geez, not in front of the kid," and—even though New York Giants was yelling back, "See, I told you she was one of them"—the laundry owner did nothing worse than clap his hand over her mouth to muffle her noise. He started dragging her backward, which she took to mean that they would continue to beat their prisoner but they wouldn't force her to watch.

She tried to bite the owner's hand, but it was sweaty and slippery, and she did little more than pinch him.

"Sidowski!" the owner hissed—another name to remember, along with Roth and Ethan Bryne, if she ever *did* make it to the police. "Knock it off!"

Kerry stopped struggling when Sidowski stepped reluctantly back from their prisoner. Kerry was amazed that she had accomplished even that.

"She tried to bite me," the owner told the others, holding up his hand.

Sidowski took a step toward Kerry, looking ready to yank her head off, but the owner held him back with his other hand on his chest, still holding the bitten hand up. "Look," he said. "Look."

What's he complaining about? Kerry thought. She hadn't even broken the skin or drawn blood.

But perhaps that was the point, for Sidowski backed off.

"See," the laundry owner said. "Just a kid." He grabbed hold of Kerry's shoulders and shook her. "You don't understand," he said to her. "He isn't human. He isn't alive."

"What?"

Kerry was still looking at Sidowski, but the owner said, "*Him,*" nodding toward Ethan Bryne.

"What?" she repeated.

"He's a vampire," the owner answered. "One of the living dead. He kills people to feed on their blood."

Their prisoner shook his head, wearing an expression of horror that probably mirrored her own.

Roth took him roughly by the jaw, forcing back his lips to reveal canine teeth that were slightly longer and sharper than normal but certainly nothing to get alarmed about.

A vampire, Kerry thought. *They think he's a vampire, and they're hoping very hard that I'm not one, too.*

It wasn't enough to step into the middle of what looked to be a ritual execution between rival gangs or druggies or international terrorists. She had to fall into a nest of grade-A crazies.

CHAPTER TWO

H E'S A VAMPIRE," Kerry repeated in a noncommittal
tone. Best not to let on that she knew they were out
of their minds.

Roth and the owner of the Quick-Clean Laundry both
nodded. Sidowski was watching her closely, waiting—she
could tell—for her to slip up and prove that she, too, was
one. Ethan, their bruised and bloodied vampire, was looking
at her with an expression of dazed desperation. Kerry wondered if he had a concussion and how likely he was to go
into shock from his injuries. Somehow, despite the mind-
numbing panic, she remembered that they kept talking about
morning, and that they had called for a video camera. Things
began to fall into place.

"You're going to keep him here till dawn," she said. "See if the rising sun . . . What? Causes him to melt? Burst into flame? *What?*"

Perhaps they thought she was making fun of their beliefs. They just looked at her with those appraising expressions.

She didn't dare vocalize the other. She didn't dare ask, *Or do you plan to put a stake through his heart?*

"Whatever you think he's done—," she started, then quickly amended it to the less judgmental, "whatever he *has* done, is there any reason we can't do something to try to stop him from bleeding to death between now and morning?"

Roth snorted. "Not likely. He's not that badly hurt. This is an act for your benefit."

Kerry moved to get to her feet, but the laundry owner put his hands down heavily on her shoulders, and Sidowski swept open his New York Giants jacket to reveal a gun nestled in a holster under his arm, a blatant reminder that they were men to be taken seriously.

"I just"—her voice was trembling as though she were talking through the spinning blades of an electric fan—"I wanted to get some of the paper towels from the desk. To try to stop the bleeding."

"He'll survive," Sidowski said. "Vampires are stronger than normal people."

The owner released the pressure on her shoulders. "Let her feel she's doing something useful," he told them. "Maybe it'll keep her from doing something stupid."

"Thank you," Kerry said meekly.

But Sidowski didn't move out of her way, which was probably meant to show her he disapproved, and she had to walk around him. Still, the advantage was that when she reached the desk, all he could see was her back.

She hadn't been planning anything in the nature of what any of the three of them could possibly call "something stupid," but as soon as she got to the desk she saw the ashtray into which she'd dropped the razor blade she'd found on the floor under the counter. Without any clear thought of what she would do with the blade but realizing that she'd probably never have a better chance to get it—knowing that if she hesitated, if she glanced to see if anybody was watching, she'd be caught—she reached for the roll of paper towels, sweeping her fingers through the ashtray on the way.

Though the blade sliced her fingertips, she worked at keeping her face blank. They would hurt worse later, she knew, but for the moment she kept moving till she had the towels. She pressed her fingers as tightly as she could into the roll of paper, trying to hide and at the same time stop the bleeding.

Turning, she found herself face-to-face with the laundry owner.

Now you've done it, she thought and braced herself for . . . she wasn't sure what, but she figured it would hurt a great deal.

He stepped out of her way, however, going around her. *The desk,* she realized with a sigh that she quickly tried to disguise as a sniffle. He had been heading for the desk—and not her—all along. He righted the chair that had tipped when Roth pulled her out from under there, and he sat down, opening a drawer.

Kerry hesitated, still standing closer to the desk than to Ethan. *Sitting down is good,* she told herself. *Sitting down is more relaxed and means he's less likely to hurt us.*

Unless, of course, he had a gun in the drawer.

Instead of a gun, the owner pulled out his Bible. Either

his place was well marked or he just opened to a random page and started reading.

Maybe he was trying to find guidance, Kerry thought. She hoped he had opened to the part that said "Thou shalt not kill."

Or maybe he was trying to look up justification for what they were planning. Not likely he could find that, she thought. But who knew how he could twist things? And besides, the Old Testament laws were strict and, in some cases, strange. Unbidden the thought came to her: *An eye for an eye, a tooth for a tooth*. If they thought Ethan was a murderous vampire, they would certainly take that as justification for killing him. Kerry fervently hoped the laundry owner would stick to the New Testament, which she remembered as being more lenient.

Mercifully, neither of the others tried to stop or delay her as she marched purposefully to Ethan and knelt before him. She ripped off a sheet of toweling and immediately and none too gently dabbed at the wound at his temple, eager to have blood on the towel, on her hand, before anybody noticed she, too, was bleeding and wondered why.

Ethan flinched from her rough ministrations.

"Sorry," she muttered, catching her first good look at his nasty cut. The area around it was already swelling and turning purple. *Easy*, she warned her stomach. It wouldn't do her Florence Nightingale routine any good if she passed out or upchucked now. *I hate this*, she thought frantically. *If there was anybody else here that could take charge, anybody* . . .

"It's all right," Ethan told her, sounding calmer than he had any right to.

Kerry's eyes shifted to his for a second.

This was no time to get herself distracted just because he

was good looking and trying to put on a brave front for her.

The towel was sloppy with blood already, his and hers, and she let the razor blade fall into it before she lightly crumpled it and shoved it into her jacket pocket, as though to get it out of the way. She hastily mopped up some more blood and put that sheet into her pocket, too. With the third, she was able to catch a glimpse of her fingers. The razor blade had cut two of them, but the bleeding seemed to be slowing down. She pressed the fourth sheet against his head with the two injured fingers—not daring to press against the actual wound, which would hurt, only near it. Every time she glanced at Ethan, he was watching her with those wary eyes. Which might mean that he could tell she was up to something and was afraid that she was going to get them both killed in the very near future, or it might mean that the blows to his head and the loss of blood had him confused enough to worry she was working with his captors. Or, more likely, the whole side of his head throbbed, and she was just making it worse.

Hold on, she wished at him. *I don't know exactly what I'm doing, but I'm trying to help.* Out loud she asked him, "Are you all right? Can you make it till dawn?"

He nodded, still looking—Kerry feared—awfully wobbly.

In a disgusted tone of voice, Sidowski swore and said, "This is the most ridiculous—"

—at the same moment Ethan shifted position.

Kerry knew exactly what he was doing. He'd been in the same kneeling position all along. His legs had to be cramping up, even not counting that one of them was injured. And he was tied to the laundry tub, which should be clear indication to all that he wasn't going far.

But Sidowski took the slight movement as a sign of intent

19

to escape. Or he just used it as an excuse. He kicked Ethan in the chest and Kerry heard his head crack yet again against the laundry tub.

Ethan clenched his jaw—against an outcry of pain or just trying to maintain consciousness, Kerry couldn't tell. His head bowed submissively, he took a couple deep breaths before getting out the barest whisper: "I just need to move my leg. Please."

"Poor thing," Sidowski said, not even sneering or sounding angry. Just cold hatred in that voice.

Ethan glanced at Sidowski with a look that cut through the hazy befuddlement, a look that all but shouted, *If I were a vampire, I'd rip out your throat.*

Or maybe it was just Kerry's interpretation of what he *should* be feeling.

In the next instant he closed his eyes and he asked, not quite begging but with a desperate edge, "May I—please— move my legs?"

Kerry looked over her shoulder to the laundry owner, who was still sitting at the desk, still holding his Bible, though the commotion had caused him to look up. "It's not like he can get away," she pointed out.

Nobody said anything.

Which, eventually, Ethan took as permission. Wincing, he leaned back and simultaneously raised himself the inch or so that the rope permitted, then gingerly managed to get his right leg out from under him and swing it around to the front.

That was the injured one. Very obviously the injured one. The whole side of his jeans was torn and bloody, from the knee down.

Ethan took a few seconds to catch his breath before moving, with a singular lack of grace, to get his other leg out from under.

Kerry felt a dizzy sympathetic reaction. "I'm going to get up now," she announced, not wanting to take Sidowski by surprise. She indicated the fistful of towels in her hand. "I just want to wet these down."

The laundry owner had resumed reading his Bible, which made Kerry so furious she wanted to knock it out of his hands and rip it up in front of his face, though she'd never had these violent inclinations toward the Bible before. Roth had moved to the main entrance, peeking out into the street from between the slats of the blinds. So she got up with only Sidowski to worry about and went to the drinking fountain, where she figured the water would be coldest and most likely to numb pain.

There was a wastepaper basket next to the fountain, where she emptied her jacket pocket of all but the towel with the razor. With these guys having vampires on the mind, she didn't want them speculating why she'd want to hold on to bloody towels.

She wet the fresh towels using her left hand, so as not to get the fingers of her right hand bleeding again. By the time she made it back to Ethan, he had gotten himself resettled. He had his left knee up and was resting his head against it. The injured right leg was stretched out in front of him.

"This is probably going to hurt," she warned.

Like he wouldn't have guessed already.

Sidowski swore again. "You think he's just some poor kid we took it in our heads to beat up on?" he demanded. "You think he's on the verge of dying because we pulled him off his bike and he got a couple cuts and bruises?"

"I don't know," Kerry said, not wanting to argue.

"He broke Ken's neck!" Sidowski shouted—Kerry jumped at the violence of his accompanying gesture. "Just like that."

Ethan's half-bewildered gaze went from Kerry to Sidowski back to Kerry. "No," he whispered. "There were only the three of them—"

Sidowski gave him another vicious kick.

"Three," Ethan gasped again.

Sidowski kicked him again.

Ethan began coughing, great wracking coughs that brought up blood.

"Stop it!" Kerry grabbed instinctively at Sidowski's arm.

Though Kerry had always thought of herself as strong and able to take care of herself, Sidowski effortlessly swept her back and hurled her to the floor.

Momentarily stunned, she knew she should roll herself into a protective ball but couldn't collect herself enough to do it. She was wide open if Sidowski chose to kick her. But he chose to kick Ethan yet again.

"Stop it!" the owner urged in a frantic whisper. But he didn't really mean it, or he would have put the book down, he'd have gotten to his feet. Instead, he just said, "Sidowski, stop it!"

That isn't going to stop him, Kerry thought. Sidowski was the kind of person who was proud in the conviction that nobody could give him orders. Clearly, he was tired of the others telling him to wait till morning, and he was going to beat Ethan until he died. There was nothing the owner would do to stop it; there was certainly nothing she could do; and Roth—

But it was Roth who *did* stop it. Roth, standing by the

door, peeking through the blinds, hissed, "Somebody's coming."

The owner finally closed his Bible. "Marcia?" he asked.

Even before he shook his head, Kerry knew that Roth wouldn't have said "Somebody" if it was one of their own.

Sidowski knew it, too—probably even the owner knew it—but Sidowski said, "No time. Not even if she found the damn batteries at home." He pulled his gun from under his arm and placed it directly against the side of Ethan's head. "Vampire or not," he said, "it'll make an awful mess."

Ethan closed his eyes and didn't make a sound, doubled over in pain as he was.

Somebody pulled on the locked door, twice, then rapped knuckles on the glass.

"Police?" the owner asked Roth in a hushed voice, frozen where he was.

Kerry thought of her slipshod parking job and fervently hoped it *was* the police.

But Roth answered, whispering also, "Customers. They're carrying laundry."

Not the police, and not Dad, either. *But Dad isn't someone to wish for,* she told herself. She fought away a mental picture of him bursting into the place ready to yell at her and finding Sidowski instead.

The owner was asking, "Do you think they heard—"

The customers knocked again.

Roth shook his head. "They probably saw me looking out, though."

"Hey," a voice called. *College girl,* Kerry thought. And even though just the one word had been spoken, she could tell: one who'd been drinking.

There was some giggling from outside. Two girls. The second one said, "Let us in. This is an emergency."

The owner raised his voice. "We're closed."

"It's an emergency," the first girl echoed her companion. "Tonya barfed on my bed, and I don't have any extra blankets."

"We're closed," the owner repeated.

" 'Twenty-four-hour laundry,' " the second girl said. "Says it right here on the door. And on the sign. And on the window. What the hell is this? You on a twenty-five-hour day?"

"The machines are broken," the owner called out. "The pipes are frozen. No water. We're closed."

One of the girls kicked the door. "Says twenty-four hours right on the goddamn door," she muttered.

But Kerry could hear them moving away, heard the car doors open and slam shut. Several times. The engine roared to life and the girls took off, squealing the car's tires to show their disdain.

Slowly, reluctantly, Sidowski lowered his gun. He didn't put it away. He looked as though he was considering taking up again where he'd left off. Like he was evaluating pistol-whipping versus kicking.

Roth said, "Why don't you just leave him alone? You're making the girl crazy; you're making everybody jumpy. He isn't going to say anything worth hearing till we put the fear of dawn in him."

"But he keeps—"

"Put the gag back on him, then," Roth snapped.

"No," Kerry said. "He'll choke." Ethan had managed to hold back his coughing while the girls were at the door, but he'd started again. For the moment he wasn't bringing up blood, but that could change, especially if Sidowski resumed kicking him.

"I think we should keep the two of them apart," the owner suggested.

"I think we should keep the two of them real close by," Sidowski countered.

The owner put his Bible back in the drawer. "I'm going out for some fresh air." He slammed the drawer shut to show he was upset at how things were going.

Big deal, Kerry thought. *He disapproves of Sidowski beating Ethan to death, but all he'll do is leave so he doesn't have to watch.* Surely that wasn't what all that reading had told him to do.

Sidowski grabbed his arm. "Don't be an idiot," he said.

"I'll be right outside," the owner told him, "waiting for Marcia."

"Let him go," Roth said.

Sidowski held on a moment longer, as if to show that—however the evening had started—he was taking no orders from the owner and he was taking no orders from Roth.

Kerry waited till after the owner slammed the door behind him so that they wouldn't think she was trying to use him as a diversion. Then she got up, slowly, so they could see she wasn't trying anything, and got a cup from the dispenser and filled it at the drinking fountain.

She suspected Sidowski was considering knocking it out of her hand, but Roth said, calmly, "Just leave them alone. She'll see soon enough."

Sidowski jammed the gun back in its holster.

Kerry knelt beside Ethan and held the cup to his lips, her hand shaking so much he was lucky to get any water at all.

He was watching her over the rim of the paper cup. People in movies were adept at passing along silent secret messages with their eyes, but she couldn't even be sure if he was trying to tell her something. After rinsing out his mouth, he spat the bloody water onto the floor, which was pretty much all he could do. Given the circumstances—what they were accusing him of—the last thing he should do was swallow it. But he spat to the left, in the direction of Sidowski, which couldn't have been coincidence no matter how lightheaded he was: dangerous, foolhardy provocation.

"Later," Sidowski promised equably.

Ethan took the rest of the water, and this time he swallowed it.

"Do you want some more?" Kerry asked.

He shook his head. "Thank you." His voice was a husky whisper. He leaned back wearily against the laundry tub, looking shaken. Things had probably caught up with him; he'd realized the risk he'd taken, to no possible advantage.

Kerry picked up the wet paper towels she'd dropped when she'd attempted to stop Sidowski from beating him. She sighed, looking at Ethan's injured leg. Mom had always been good at medical emergencies—levelheaded and not the least bit squeamish. Kerry knew enough to see that his pants leg needed to be cut away, but the men were no more likely to let her have scissors or a knife than to call for an ambulance. "Motorcycle?" she asked, remembering Sidowski saying they'd pulled him off his bike and remembering a much, much less serious version of this same type of injury when she'd been about ten years old and had fallen off a skateboard. She recognized the effects of a high-speed skid on gravel.

Ethan took in a sharp breath as she laid the towel on his leg. "Bicycle," he corrected her.

She was about to tell him that he was crazy to be riding a bicycle in December, vampire hunters notwithstanding, even if it hadn't snowed yet. But then she took into account the fact that he was wearing only a sweatshirt while the rest of them all had jackets. A bicycle was probably all the transportation a college freshman could afford. No telling how he'd make do once winter set in seriously.

Sidowski finally got bored enough to back away. He hoisted himself up to sit on the counter a whole seven, maybe eight feet distant. Still, he watched every move they made. Roth continued to look out into the street from his position by the front door.

"You staying at the college?" she asked Ethan, simply to say something, to keep his mind—and hers—off of what she was doing. Out of the corner of her eye she saw him shake his head; he was biting his lip, concentrating on not shouting or smacking her clumsy hands away from him. Then she remembered he couldn't smack her hands away, no matter how much she hurt him. "Sorry," she whispered.

He nodded.

She went to get some fresh towels. So he was older than she had assumed, she thought. Only juniors and seniors were allowed off-campus housing. *Stop it*, she told herself. They were in too much trouble for her to be concerned because he was too old for her.

She was uncomfortably hot in her jacket but didn't dare unzip it. For one thing, she wasn't wearing a bra. For another, Sidowski would probably take the message on her nightshirt, IF IT'S MORNING, DON'T TALK TO ME, as a clear confession that she was a vampire.

When she got back to Ethan, he was leaning his head against his upraised good knee.

"Do you want me to stop?" she asked.

He shook his head, but it seemed more an I-don't-care gesture than an acknowledgment that her first aid was helping.

She knelt beside him, hesitating, unsure whether she was making things worse rather than better.

27

He turned his face to her without lifting his head, making it harder, should Sidowski be listening, to be overheard. "I'm not what they say I am," he whispered. "I'm not a vampire."

Kerry bent over his leg and whispered also. "I know that." She was chagrined that he felt he had to tell her.

"I never saw any fourth man," Ethan said. "I didn't kill anybody."

"*Shh*," she warned, lest their whispering attract attention. Obviously Sidowski could see that they were talking, but if he knew it was more than *I hope this doesn't hurt*, he was likely to interfere again.

But Ethan wasn't finished. "They're going to kill me," he whispered.

Kerry shook her head. "Once they see that the sunlight doesn't affect you—"

"They're going to find some excuse," Ethan insisted. "The sky is going to be too overcast, or it needs to be the noonday sun, or . . . I don't know, but they're going to find some excuse and they're going to kill me."

Kerry had been so intent on surviving till dawn, she didn't know what to say now that he told her dawn wouldn't be the end of it. Ethan flinched as she pressed too heavily. "Sorry," she said automatically.

"Besides," he whispered, "I think they have some sort of idea that I can tell them where other vampires are. I think they figure that the closer it is to dawn, the more frantic I'll become, and they might be able to . . . get me to give them some names and addresses."

Kerry bit at her lip, suspecting he was right, suspecting that *getting* him to cooperate would probably involve a good deal more than just the threat of sunlight. "No," she said. "They've sent for a video camera. They won't kill you. They

28

want recorded proof that the sun will do that." But even as she said it, she knew they didn't think they *could* kill him. Just rough him up. Cause him some pain. They'd keep on beating him, thinking that the sun would destroy his body and once they had that on film, nobody would question what they'd done before. She glanced at Sidowski, who was watching attentively. She didn't think he could hear what she and Ethan were saying, but she couldn't be sure. "What should I do?" she asked Ethan in an even lower whisper.

"I truly don't think you're in danger," Ethan said. "Just don't keep riling them."

"I'm not," she protested.

"Keep away from me. Do whatever they say. But as soon as it gets to be dawn—*as soon*—demand to be released: that's the time to make a fuss. Once they realize they've killed a mortal man, they're going to know they have to cover up."

Kill the witness, was what he meant. Kerry was finding it hard to breathe.

"My name is Ethan Bryne," he repeated. "I live at my uncle's house at 3747 Brockport–Bergen Road, but he's out of the country. Nobody's going to miss me until I don't show up for classes for a couple days."

Kerry bit her lip, forcing herself not to cry. Ethan was making plans for her, trying to see to her safety because there was no hope for him.

But Sidowski saw her. "What the hell is he telling you?" he demanded, sliding off the counter.

"Nothing," she and Ethan said simultaneously.

Sidowski took a step forward, but Roth saved Ethan for the second time that night. Roth announced, "Marcia's pulling up."

29

THE NUMBER OF bad guys in the room was about to increase. If she was ever going to do anything, Kerry knew that now was her last chance.

As Sidowski turned and headed for the back door, she whispered into Ethan's ear, "Lean forward," and shoved against his shoulder to get him as far away from the laundry tub as she could. Ethan was between her and the door, some protection against Sidowski's seeing what she was up to. But if Roth turned from the front window, it would be all over.

The razor blade nicked her fingers again as she got it unwrapped from the paper towel and out of her pocket. No time to think of that. She could hear a car pulling up in front of the laundry.

Behind Ethan's back, it was a case of good news / bad news. The good news was that the laundry owner had secured Ethan to the tub's leg by wrapping a rope around the first rope, the one that already bound his wrists. This meant all she had to do was cut through the rope that held his hands behind his back, and the other would automatically fall free. The bad news was that whichever one of the men had tied Ethan's wrists together in the first place had wrapped the rope around both wrists three or four times, crisscrossing in between.

There wasn't time. There just wasn't time to cut through all that rope. Kerry froze, staring at the impossible mess.

She heard Roth, at the front window, mutter, "Geez, Marcia, give it a rest." He rapped his knuckles loudly on the glass. "Just park the damn thing!" he shouted, and Kerry took in the fact that she hadn't heard the car engine turn off yet.

She's having a hard time parallel parking, Kerry realized. She could sympathize. But even better, Marcia was going by daytime-everything's-normal parking rules and didn't want to block the fire hydrant.

Maybe there was a chance after all. Kerry began sawing at the rope where it passed over Ethan's right wrist. She ran the risk of cutting him badly, but if she worked at the tangle of strands in the middle, there was no chance at all.

The car engine turned off, just as Kerry made it through one thickness of the rope. Only three more to go.

A car door opened, then another one, so rapidly afterward that Kerry guessed the laundry owner had come around the front and was opening the passenger door to get the long-awaited video camera.

Halfway through the second rope, both doors slammed shut. She pressed harder and the blade slipped, gouging

Ethan's wrist. He jumped but didn't make a sound. She froze. Blood, a shocking amount of it, ran down his hands and onto the floor. Slitting their wrists was a way people committed suicide. How long did it take for them to bleed to death?

"Keep going," he whispered at her. Could he tell how serious an injury his would-be rescuer had just inflicted on him? Not that it made any difference at this point.

She gritted her teeth and set the razor blade once more on the rope, though the blood made it hard to see what she was doing.

She felt the second strand give as Sidowski opened the laundry's back door, and she had already started on the third when he finished saying, "About time."

But then Sidowski turned and saw her. "Hey!" he yelled. "What are you doing?"

Kerry sliced the rest of the way through the rope. Ethan took in a sharp breath as she laid open his wrist a second time.

All for nothing, she realized, with another strand left and no way to cut through it with Sidowski about ten quick steps away. She dropped the razor blade to the floor and wiped her left hand, the less bloody of the two, on her pants leg. "Nothing," she said. "Just getting my brother's bear." She reached her left hand for Footy, who'd been kicked in that general direction when she'd first dropped him; he was now sort of near where she was sitting.

Not near enough for anybody to be fooled, of course.

She picked up the bear and held him up for them to see: Roth behind her, and in front Sidowski, the laundry owner, and a woman with blond hair piled up on her head the way only hairdressers ever wear it. Kerry could see Ethan's blood under her fingernails. The others probably couldn't, but it didn't make any difference.

Sidowski took a step toward her. And another. Kerry could make out the individual motions, as though everything had slowed. And yet, by Sidowski's third step Kerry saw that she had vastly miscalculated and that it would take more like five steps rather than ten for him to reach them, but at that point Ethan jerked his hands apart, the final strand of rope coming loose.

On Sidowski's fourth step, Ethan swept up the razor blade. Considering the amount of blood already on his hands, there was no way to tell if he cut himself further, but Kerry figured he pretty much had to.

From the other side, Roth yelled, "He's loose!" which the others probably couldn't see yet—

—as Sidowski's fifth step brought him alongside Ethan. But he hadn't realized Ethan was loose, and he hadn't seen the razor yet. He'd been heading for her, one hand just starting to move, to reach down and over Ethan to grab her hair. Kerry could see it in his face as he took in Roth's words, as he took in the changed situation.

Kerry was sure Ethan was going to use the razor blade on Sidowski: slash open arm or leg or belly or face—the kind of thing that during movies she'd always hide her eyes for. Not that she saw he had much choice.

But Ethan had gotten his good leg under him, and he jabbed his left elbow into Sidowski's groin with all the force the momentum of getting up gave him. Sidowski doubled over, and Ethan hit him again, this time on the chin.

Ethan was on his feet faster than Kerry would have thought possible, and the one he went after was not Sidowski, in a helpless heap on the floor, but Marcia.

Marcia yelped but didn't have time to struggle before he was behind her, left arm around her waist, right hand holding the blade to her throat, while from his slashed wrist blood spread alarmingly quickly over the front of her powder blue ski jacket.

"Back off," he warned, his voice still barely more than a whisper.

Roth, who'd almost made it to where Kerry still knelt on the floor, said, "Just take it easy. She's been home all evening. She hasn't done anything to hurt you."

The laundry owner dropped the video camera. *Shock,* Kerry thought, seeing his face. But the sudden noise made Ethan jerk his arm tighter around Marcia's neck. Marcia squealed in anticipation of pain. From where she was, Kerry could see that Ethan hadn't cut her; the blood was still all his. Off to the side, the laundry owner—Marcia *must be* Mrs. Laundry Owner—cried out, "No!" Roth took a step closer, but Ethan wasn't as distracted as all that.

"I have," Ethan warned softly, "nothing to lose."

"Roth," the laundry owner pleaded.

For one incredibly long second they all stood there watching each other, gauging intent, searching for weaknesses. Then Roth stepped back.

Sidowski had regained enough breath to start swearing.

Ethan ignored him. "Kerry, you drove?"

She nodded.

"You still have the keys?"

She had to think about it. She was still kneeling on the floor, Footy in her left hand. The keys turned up in her jeans pocket. She stuffed Footy into her jacket pocket and stood.

"Open the passenger door," Ethan told her. "Start the car. All right?"

34

Somehow, after all this, he was worried that she would leave without him? "All right," she assured him.

"The rest of you, sit down," he ordered.

She walked past Sidowski; past Ethan holding Marcia the hairdresser, who looked as scared as Kerry had been; past the laundry owner. She tried not to feel sorry for Marcia. *They've been threatening me for hours,* she told herself. For Marcia, it was only going to last a couple minutes. And Ethan wasn't a crazy: Ethan would threaten, but he wouldn't really hurt her.

Though, of course, Marcia had no way of knowing that.

Kerry ran out the back door, around the corner, and into the street. She opened the passenger door first, then went around to the other side, got in, and started the engine.

Ethan came around the corner, half dragging Marcia.

Kerry threw the car into reverse to get closer, sweeping aside a KEEP OUR TOWN CLEAN garbage can with the open door.

Ethan shoved Marcia away from him, hard enough that she stumbled and fell. Kerry tried not to think about it, tried not to wonder if shoving her was all he did. Then he jumped into the car. Kerry floored the accelerator even before he got the door closed.

Somehow she missed rear-ending Marcia's station wagon. In the rearview mirror she saw the sidewalk flooded by light as the laundry's front door burst open. Somebody—it had to be the laundry owner—headed immediately for the fallen Marcia.

They were about a block away when she heard the crack of a gun. She ducked instinctively, even though she knew that if the bullet were going to hit, it would have hit already. She had a moment to think that if she brought the car home with a bullet hole, her father would kill her. Then there were two more shots, one after the other.

"We're too far away," Ethan assured her.

He had to be right because the windows had all survived.

"Good," she said, momentarily slowing just enough so that the car wouldn't become airborne when they hit the bump right before the bridge. "You didn't . . ." She floored the accelerator despite the red traffic light and glanced at him once they made it through the mercifully empty inter-section in front of the minimart. He was still waiting. ". . . kill her? Did you?"

"No," he said, and shook his head for emphasis. "No." He leaned forward, putting his head between his knees. "God," he whispered.

Kerry took a corner fast enough to squeal and slide. She slowed down, realizing that at this hour of the night, on these roads, she was more likely to attract the attention of pursuers by speeding than by going the speed limit.

She went around two more corners, quick rights, so that they would be headed back into town rather than going down country roads where it'd be miles between turnoffs. She knew she'd never have the nerve to outlast a determined driver in the kind of high-speed chase people have on TV.

"Ethan," she said then because he hadn't moved in all this while. "*Ethan.*"

He raised his head. Slightly.

"Are you all right?" She wasn't that experienced a driver. It was hard to take her eyes off the road.

He nodded. Sat back. Got a handkerchief from his jeans pocket and started tying it around his wrist. "What are you doing?" he asked, finally noticing that they'd returned almost to where they'd started.

"They saw us head off the other way," she said. "Which is north. Hopefully they won't think to look for us to the south." That was assuming, of course, that she wouldn't pass them going the other direction, and that—if she did—they wouldn't recognize her car.

Ethan nodded again. With his left hand and his teeth he managed to get the handkerchief tied around his right wrist.

She dared another, longer glance at him, unsure whether this inadequate-looking first aid would be enough to stop the bleeding. It seemed to be. For the moment, at least.

And then they were passing by the laundry again. The door was still open, but in the glimpse she had, it didn't look as if anybody was still there. Definitely nobody on the sidewalk in front. She didn't think anybody was around the corner. No station wagon. No police, either, despite all their noise. Almost as though she'd imagined it all. Except for the pale and bleeding young man beside her.

"Is the campus clinic open twenty-four hours a day?" she asked. It was closer than the hospital.

"I don't know," Ethan said. "I've never had to use it before."

"Or should we go to the police first?"

Ethan considered. "Clinic." He saw the anxious glance she gave him. "I'm all right," he assured her. "They can call the police from there."

She didn't think he looked all right. She didn't think she'd ever seen anybody look so pale, except for her Aunt Fern. And the only time she'd seen Aunt Fern had been at Aunt Fern's funeral.

Kerry turned down the street that led to the campus. "You're going to have to direct me," she told him. "I'm not too familiar with the campus. And I've never driven at night before."

Damn it! she thought, seeing the sharp look he gave her. *Why in the world did I have to volunteer that information?*

"You don't have a driver's license," he guessed.

She'd always been a terrible liar: her face gave away what her voice didn't. So she didn't even try. She just shook her head.

He leaned back again, still looking at her. "Kerry," he said gently, "just how old are you?"

"Sixteen." They were going slowly enough that she could look at him. If he was older than she'd first thought, evidently she was younger than he'd guessed. *Me and my big mouth.*

"Left," he told her without enough warning, so that she turned too sharply and ran over the curb.

"Sorry," she muttered.

He leaned forward to point. "After this building."

That time he had given her enough warning—except that she thought it was one big building with a Dumpster between the wings, and by the time she saw the driveway beyond the Dumpster, she was already past it.

"Just pull over," Ethan told her.

She did, pulling over to the left because that was where the building was, before she remembered it was a two-way street.

"Sorry," she said again.

"It's all right." He leaned back again, and she realized he was laughing.

"Sorry," she said automatically, not even knowing why. She turned the engine off abruptly. *He* was laughing at her and *she* was apologizing?

He could tell she was angry. "No, Kerry. It's just relief." All trace of laughter was gone. His voice was back to being almost a whisper. "I'm sorry. I owe you my life."

We both almost got ourselves killed, she thought. *Him especially, but it could have been both of us.* Now, of all times, she started to shake.

Ethan slid over and put his arm around her.

"I'm sorry," she said yet again. This time she knew why: for being so foolish *after* it was all over. By the glow of the lights in the parking lot across the street she could see him fight back a grin. Then he kissed her, lightly, on the forehead. She told herself it was camouflage, to disguise the fact that he was laughing at her again. But it was very sweet anyway.

Ethan moved back to his side of the seat, a clear and strong indication that one kiss was all he intended.

Kerry hadn't made up her mind yet, but she certainly wasn't going to throw herself at him. "I'll come around and help you," she offered, unsure how steady he'd be once he stood up.

"I can make it on my own," he said, which seemed one of those silly male things, but then he added, "If you come in, you're going to be in a lot of trouble."

"I'm going to be in trouble in any case," she pointed out.

Ethan opened the car door without answering. He walked around to her side, favoring the injured right leg, but when she started to get out, he shooed her over to the passenger side.

"What are you doing?" she asked as he climbed into the driver's seat.

He held out his hand for the car keys. "Why were you there," he asked, "at the laundry?"

She was tempted to take Footy out of her pocket and beat him with it. "Doesn't anybody listen? To get my brother's bear that he left behind this afternoon."

He cut her off before she could add anything else. "How

do you think your parents are going to take to that as a motive for being out at this hour, in their car, on a learner's permit? How do you think the police are going to react?"

"My *father*," Kerry said, "is going to kill me. The police will probably take away my learner's permit and put me in jail until I'm fifty years old. But since I'll be dead already, that won't matter."

"I'm going to drive you home," Ethan said. "No, actually, I'm going to drive me to my house. You'll have to drive home from there. I'll take my uncle's car and go to the police. I'll tell them that those guys jumped me when I went into the laundry and that I managed to break away on my own. I won't mention you at all."

"Ethan. That won't work. Not only did they see me, they know who I am."

"Do you think they're going to volunteer the information that they were terrorizing a sixteen-year-old girl? They'll already be up for assault and battery. Conspiracy to commit murder. If they bring you into it . . . People go crazy when other people hurt kids. If I don't mention you, they won't mention you."

Kerry thought about it, wishing that it could be that easy.

"I'll only tell them about you as a last resort," he promised.

Still she hesitated. She'd never be able to pull it off. She'd have to clean up Ethan's blood, which had gotten all over the seat, and her jeans had a bloody smear where she'd wiped her hand before grabbing Footy. Would Ian have gotten Dad up when she didn't come home? Did Dad know already?

Ethan was watching her, looking a lot stronger now that

he'd caught his breath. He was terribly brave, Kerry thought.

She dropped the keys into his outstretched palm, knowing she'd have to wash them off, too, now, and the steering wheel. It'd never work.

"We can try," she said.

CHAPTER FOUR

KERRY KNEW THE street where Ethan lived—it was behind the supermarket where she worked Fridays after
school and on Saturday afternoons. She even recognized
Ethan's uncle's house. A sprawling Victorian with a wrap-
around porch, angled roofs and dormers, and turrets topped
by conical towers, it was the one about which she always
said, "Someday, when I'm rich and famous, I'm going to buy
that house." The thing that set it apart from the other fine
old Victorians in Brockport was the enormous yard, never
subdivided in the crunch for land. Every spring and summer
there were lovely flowers and bushes, so this yard always
seemed to have more color and life than anyplace else.

"Does your uncle do all the gardening himself?" Kerry asked as Ethan pulled into the driveway.

Ethan gave her a startled look, as though wondering what kind of gardening she thought anyone would be doing in December. Before she could clarify, he said, "No. He hires in people." And she realized it wasn't so much her question that had taken him aback but that something was distracting him.

"What is it?" she asked as he shifted the car into reverse.

The car lurched backward as he stepped hard on the accelerator. But an instant later, he hit the brake. "Sorry," he said. "I know I didn't leave the light on, but it's all right."

Good thing they weren't dependent on *her* reflexes. Kerry had seen the light in one of the front windows and hadn't given it a thought. She had even seen the door open, but her only reaction had been her heart sinking when she saw that it was an attractive woman. *Silly*, she told herself. She had no claim on Ethan.

Ethan pulled the car up till it was opposite the porch, and he turned off the engine.

Close up, the woman was about Kerry's mother's age, but Kerry very much doubted she'd turn out to be Ethan's aunt. For one thing, Ethan had mentioned only an uncle; for another, she just didn't *look* like anybody's aunt, standing there on the porch in stocking feet, holding a glass of white wine. Kerry had seen enough of her mother's boyfriend, before they disappeared in Florida, to know that some women prefer younger men. This woman leaned on the side railing and gave Kerry a smile that was probably about as friendly as the one Kerry returned.

"Well, well," the woman said, never taking her gaze off

Kerry as Ethan got out of the car, "so much for dropping in unannounced."

Kerry hesitated to open the car door; she'd have to step closer to the woman on the porch before she could step away. But her reluctance put her in a worse position, because Ethan came around to open the door for her, as though that had been what she was waiting for, which made the woman raise her eyebrows appraisingly. "She seems rather young, *mon cher*," she said as Kerry stepped out of the car, "but I'm sure you know what you're doing. Just let me get my shoes."

Kerry felt her cheeks go hot. Thinking that Ethan was incredibly good looking, and that it was a sign from heaven that he lived in "her" house, then being disappointed to find that he apparently already had a girlfriend—a much older girlfriend—this was not the same as planning to spend the night with him. Or anybody, at this point in her life.

She guessed Ethan was probably as mortified as she was. "This is Kerry Nowicki," he said hastily as the woman started to turn. "She just saved my life."

The woman turned back, looking mildly amused.

"And, Kerry, this is Regina Sloane." He hesitated before finishing, lamely, "My technical writing instructor."

Regina blew him a kiss that couldn't disguise she was miffed at how he'd chosen to identify her. *"Mon cher,"* she said again—Kerry found her use of the French endearment pretentious in the absence of a French accent—"there's a minimum number of classes you must attend before even I must penalize you."

As though she were here only to check on a truant student. And let herself into his house. And into his refrigerator. *It doesn't make any difference to me if he chooses to make out with a teacher old enough to be his mother,* Kerry thought. She fought back the little voice that argued Regina might be old enough to be *her* mother, but not Ethan's. She shrugged to show she didn't care.

"Did you walk here?" Ethan asked Regina. "Or did you drive?"

She gave him a tight smile. "Oh, I drove," she said. "My car's back by the garage." She indicated with a nod where the driveway curved around behind the house. And still no request for an explanation of what had happened.

"I'd like to get Kerry back to her home before her father catches on that she's missing," Ethan said. "And she isn't supposed to be driving without someone who has a license." Kerry noticed that he'd picked up on the fact that her mother didn't live with them. *Quick,* she thought. *As well as incredibly attractive.*

Stop it, she told herself. *As far as he's concerned, you're a kid.*

If Regina was his type, Kerry would be a kid until she hit her thirties.

"Could we use your car?" Ethan asked.

"Certainly." Regina gave another of her predatory smiles. Finally, offhandedly, she asked, "Are you going to tell me what happened?" She'd shifted her attention to Ethan now that she'd seen Kerry was no competition, and Ethan dismissed Kerry, too, with an "I'll be back in a minute," which obviously meant, *Don't come in.* Regina walked along the porch railing, keeping pace as Ethan limped down the flagstone path to the front steps.

"There'll be more time later," he said, somewhat breathlessly. He had to lean on the front post before he could make it up the three stairs.

Standing by the car, Kerry was too far away to be any help, and Regina, standing right there, didn't budge. "Nasty," she said, indicating his torn and bloody leg. She downed the rest of her wine and hurried into the house, as though the cold had suddenly seeped into her feet.

"I'll be back in a minute," Ethan told Kerry again, and he disappeared into the house behind Regina.

Standing where she was—rather, standing on tiptoe where she was—Kerry could see into one corner of the living room. Ethan might not be able to afford a jacket or a car of his own, but his uncle was certainly well off. She could see part of an Oriental rug, a grand piano, a grandfather clock, and a huge gold-framed mirror. Regina walked into the part of the room that was reflected in the mirror. She stopped abruptly and turned, and in a moment Ethan caught up.

Kerry ducked, afraid to be caught staring with her nose pressed against the glass, but then she estimated that—unless there was another mirror—she could see in better than they could see out.

When she peeked in again, the two of them were talking, though with the windows closed Kerry couldn't hear a thing. *Ha!* she thought of Regina. *Too sophisticated to care what happened, are we?* She would have loved to hear Ethan's obviously condensed story. She couldn't tell, from Regina's face, what she made of it all.

Then, suddenly, they were kissing, too fast for Kerry to catch who had made the first move. Kerry ducked again. She'd never had a teacher kiss her like that, she thought. On second thought, she'd never had a teacher she'd have *wanted* to kiss her like that. And just when she'd begun hoping that maybe she'd misinterpreted the situation.

Kerry wrapped her arms around herself, suddenly aware of the cold.

46

When she glanced in again, the mirror showed only the fireplace, flanked by leaded-glass bookcases. She'd just gotten off her tiptoes when the front door slammed and Regina came out.

No telling if she guessed Kerry had been spying. She came and leaned against the car, smoking a cigarette, never quite looking at Kerry, wearing a distant but smug smile. *What was that for?* Kerry wondered. Surely not relief? Surely somebody that gorgeous couldn't have been nervous about competition from a sixteen-year-old who didn't have any makeup and who was wearing a nightshirt that was now hanging below her jacket? More likely, it was just Regina's natural expression.

When Ethan finally came out, he'd changed clothes. Still no jacket, but he'd wrapped a fresh bandage around his right hand, and in his left he was carrying a bucket of sudsy water.

Regina moved a fraction of an inch so he could open the passenger door. Stiffly, and without a word to either of them, Ethan got down on his good knee and began scrubbing at the blood that had gotten onto the seat and floor mat. Regina pulled out another cigarette.

Even realizing that their indifference was likely only a case of not-in-front-of-the-child, Kerry felt sorry for Ethan. "Here, let me help," she offered. "You're in no shape . . ."

Ethan shook his head, giving a fleeting smile that was almost enough to make her resolve to take on Regina. But in any case, he'd brought only one rag.

She hovered uselessly, convinced she really should insist, and equally convinced Regina was silently laughing at her.

The question was: was Ethan?

He wiped down the steering wheel, inner and outer door

handles, and the dashboard. If anything, Kerry's father was going to wonder why the car was cleaner than it'd been in a long time.

Finally Ethan stood, moving slowly, favoring his injured leg more than he had been previously. He had gotten his bandage wet, and blood had seeped through onto the cuff of his gray sweater.

Kerry noticed again how pale he was. It was stupid not to have gone straight to the clinic. At the very least he should sit until he caught his breath, but Regina crushed out her latest cigarette and asked, "Ready?" Then, hardly giving him a chance if he planned to say no, she gave him a quick peck on the cheek and told Kerry, "Why don't you come in my car? I think Ethan's done a pretty good job of soaking down the passenger seat here, and there's no use in your getting a wet bottom just to be able to ride with him."

Kerry felt her cheeks go hot and red again, so she hardly glanced at Ethan to see if he'd offer any objection.

Not that she could think why he would.

He didn't.

Regina's car, parked beyond the bend in the driveway, turned out to be a red Ferrari. Somehow Kerry wasn't surprised. Impressed, despite herself, but not surprised. While she waited for Regina to lean over and unlock the passenger door, she noted that Ethan's uncle had a three-car garage and a tennis court back here. There was also a stockade fence, which probably indicated a built-in pool. The house was looking better and better. And ever more unattainable, no matter how rich and famous Kerry ever got.

"Lift the handle, sweetie," Regina said, as though she didn't realize Kerry's mind had momentarily wandered, as though she thought Kerry couldn't figure out for herself how to get into the car.

There was a man's denim jacket on the floor of the passenger's side. *Probably not Ethan's,* Kerry thought, picking it up rather than stepping on it, *or Regina would likely have taken it into the house. Just how many students does she make house calls on?* Kerry wondered.

Looking over her shoulder to back out, Regina saw Kerry holding the jacket. "Just wad it up and toss it in the back," she said.

If Regina didn't care, why should Kerry? She flung the jacket behind her.

Ethan had already backed her father's car up to, but not into, the street. He pointed to the left and then to the right, asking which way to turn.

Kerry pointed to the left, and he backed out to the right but facing left, so that they could lead.

"Where to, sweets?" Regina asked.

"Fawn Meadow Circle," Kerry said. "It's—"

"I know where it is," Regina interrupted.

That was a surprise. It wasn't in the village of Brockport itself but in a nearby development, all of which had pseudo-woodsy names like Doe Run and Meadowlark Lane. Kerry was prepared for Regina to be hesitant once she got into the development, but she wasn't even fooled by Fawn Meadow Drive, the street before Fawn Meadow Circle.

"Do you live near here?" Kerry asked, thinking that might be good news if Ethan ever visited Regina's house. She might actually get to see him again.

But Regina gave her a look that said she most definitely didn't live in this neighborhood and that Kerry was a fool to even consider she might. "Which house?" she asked, the first thing she'd said in the seven- or eight-minute drive.

"The blue two-story with the basketball hoop on the garage." Kerry figured that in this light Regina was just as likely to pull up in front of the Armendarizes' house, which, in daylight, was green.

But by chance—either that, or Regina was *very* familiar with the neighborhood—Regina found the right house.

"Thanks," Kerry mumbled, glad for an excuse to jump out of the car—to show Ethan exactly where in the driveway he should park so Dad wouldn't notice that it had been moved.

Ethan turned off the engine and got out to look at the house, which Kerry realized she should have already done. The light by the front door was on, but she'd left it that way so as not to have to find her way up a dark walk. None of the other downstairs lights were on. Upstairs, Ian's drapes were open and—though there was no sign of Ian—she could see his elephant lamp was on. But the windows of her father's room were dark. Most significantly, Kerry's father hadn't come crashing out the front door bellowing, "Where have you *been*, young lady?" so Kerry felt confident telling Ethan, "Everything's fine."

"You're sure?" he asked. "Do you want to go in, maybe flash the lights as a signal if you don't need me?"

It was, she felt, a serious offer, but she shook her head.

He handed her the keys. "I'm . . ." He seemed to search before settling on just the right word: ". . . *certain* your name is never going to come up."

Kerry shrugged, unsure how to answer. *If you say so? I hope not? Are you free the night of the junior dance?*

Unexpectedly, Ethan took her hands, leaned forward, and gave her a light kiss on the cheek. The second time tonight, and on neither occasion had she had the time or the presence of mind to respond. "You *did* save my life," he told her, smiling, his tone light but his eyes very, very serious.

Out on the street, Regina tapped her car horn. It only lasted a moment, but at two-thirty in the morning, that might just be enough to rouse the neighborhood. "*Uhm* . . . ," Kerry started.

But Ethan only waited a second to determine that she didn't, in fact, have anything to say. He smiled again as he pulled his hands from hers. "Thank you," he said, turning to head back out to the street.

Kerry hurried to the front door, flew in, turned off the light before Mrs. Armendariz could see it and say—later that morning, when Kerry's father dropped Ian off for the day—"There was some sort of commotion in front of your house last night, and your light was on. Are you letting your children run wild?" Mrs. Armendariz had a thing about single parents who let their children run wild.

Kerry went upstairs as quickly as she could without making noise. Her father's door was still closed. Ian was sprawled across his bed, asleep despite the light being left on. Kerry pulled his blanket up over him, then removed Footy from her jacket pocket and wedged the koala bear under her brother's arm. When she went to the window to shut the drapes, she saw that Regina's car was gone. "Good-bye, Ethan," she whispered. "It was nice knowing you. Bizarre, but nice."

She flicked off the light, leaving only Ian's night-light on. Then she headed for her own bed, knowing that unless something went wrong with their plan and the police came banging on her door demanding explanations, the chances were she'd never see Ethan Bryne again.

CHAPTER FIVE

K ERRY'S ALARM WENT off four hours later, but she felt as if she'd had only about fifteen minutes' sleep.

In the kitchen, her father was whistling while he poured himself a bowlful of the cereal that Kerry thought of as Bran, Twigs, and Gravel. She searched through the cupboard for anything with a lot of sugar and marshmallow shapes.

"Good morning," her father said, planting a kiss on the back of her head as they met in front of the refrigerator, he getting the skim milk and she the regular.

Kerry gave a noncommittal grunt. Under the best of circumstances, mornings were not a good time for her, and her father didn't seem to sense anything unusual now. He had the newspaper on the table, which meant he'd been outside already. Apparently Mrs. Armendariz hadn't come running out to complain, and apparently nothing was so obviously wrong with the car or its location that he commented. Kerry, who never read anything besides the comics page, tried to be unobtrusive about skimming the headlines. No story about a ring of vampire hunters being captured, nor about the police looking for a mystery girl.

Still, she didn't let herself relax. There really hadn't been time for the morning papers to get the story. They'd probably have her picture by the evening edition. If there was time after Dad left for work, she could turn on the TV and try the local news.

Ian came down without having to be carried or threatened, which was unusual, and he planted a big wet kiss on Kerry's cheek, which was downright odd. But he had the sense not to say anything about last night. He made Footy give Kerry a kiss, too, despite the fact that Kerry growled at him.

"Such a pleasant family," Dad said with a smile that was much too bright for so early in the morning.

Kerry grunted again.

Eventually Dad took Ian over to Mrs. Armendariz's. Kerry watched from behind the drape in Ian's room. Dad certainly didn't seem to take any longer than usual to drop Ian off. Maybe Mrs. Armendariz hadn't heard or seen anything last night to complain about.

Then Dad got into the car and pulled out of the driveway, drove around the circle and down the street. No hesitation that Kerry could see. *Maybe I'm going to get away with this after all,* she thought.

Yeah, right, she told herself. *More likely it's all just going to cave in later.*

ALL DAY AT school she half expected to hear her name announced over the PA system: *Kerry Nowicki, please come to the principal's office; the FBI is here to arrest you.*

In fact, it almost would have been a relief. Especially during her second period literature test on the book she had never finished. "What was the narrator's name?" she hastily asked her friend Nelle as they settled into their seats seconds before the bell. "Did she ever get a name by the end of the last chapter?"

But nobody came to fetch her during school, and when she took the bus that dropped her off at the supermarket, the police weren't waiting for her there either.

"My father call?" she asked Elaine at customer service.

Elaine glanced through the phone messages. "Nope. Were you expecting him to?"

"Not really." Kerry headed back to the lockers before Elaine could start asking questions. In the locker room, some-one had left the front section of the evening paper on the bench. That was usually world news, but if something im-portant happened locally, it'd be on the front page. Kerry thought abduction and attempted murder on Main Street should qualify as important; and even if that was too common these days, surely the fact that the criminals saw themselves as vampire hunters must be unusual enough for a mention.

Nothing.

Maybe the police hadn't released all the details yet be-cause they were still investigating. Chilling as a cold hand on the back of her spine, another thought came to her: Maybe the laundry owner and Sidowski and Roth and Marcia had gone into hiding; maybe the police hadn't been able to catch them at all. *What if they come after me?* she thought. Surely, if there hadn't been arrests, Ethan would have told the police about her so they could protect her. Wouldn't he?

She spent the next five hours unable to remember regular customers' names. She made mistakes giving change, rang up cabbage as lettuce, even overloaded cranky old Mr. Nate's shopping bag so that he complained at the office.

Finally, when her shift was over, the head cashier patted her on the shoulder and said, "Get a good night's rest for tomorrow, would you?" and she sat down by the door to wait for her father to pick her up, thinking this was the worst day she had ever lived through, even worse than last night.

After a few minutes she shouldered the backpack containing her school clothes and books and went outside, just in case her father was waiting in the parking lot, but there was no sign of him. By 8:20 she was thinking that she could have walked home, and she went back to the customer service desk to have Elaine call her house. There was no answer.

"Must have just noticed the time and he's on his way," Elaine assured her.

But those who were leaving at 8:30 cashed out, got their things from their lockers, and left, and still no sign of her father.

Kerry went back to customer service, but Elaine had gone for the night and Craig didn't allow personal phone calls. So Kerry called Mrs. Armendariz from the pay phone that was located, for some reason Kerry had never been able to figure out, near the crash and clatter of the beverage-container return center. All Mrs. Armendariz had to offer was that Kerry's father had taken a half-day's vacation from work to take Ian to the pediatrician for his four-year checkup, and he had picked up Ian shortly after noon. She hadn't noticed anything since then, and the car wasn't in the driveway.

"Thanks," Kerry said.

Something had happened, she was sure of it. Ever since Mom had left, Dad, who had never been on time in his life before, had made a strict point of being punctual. He was never more than five minutes late to pick her up, and here it was almost forty-five minutes past the time he knew she was expecting him.

It has to be the car, she thought. *Oh, please let it be car trouble, not anything to do with—*

Turning from the phone, Kerry walked smack into Ethan Bryne.

He put out a hand to steady her, and only a second later seemed to recognize who she was. "Kerry," he said. And, a moment after that, "What's the matter?"

"My father was supposed to pick me up at eight o'clock." She felt awful, because she was truly concerned about her father and Ian, and yet here she was aware that her super-market uniform of white shirt and black pants looked like a stupid tuxedo-for-girls, and her eyes were red-rimmed because she was worried. *Don't cry,* she told herself. *You don't need to cry just to prove you're more worried about him than about how you look.*

"Kerry," Ethan repeated gently.

A woman and her daughter entering the store were forced to walk around them. The little girl craned around to stare, not making any pretense of not listening.

"I'm afraid something's happened," Kerry said. "Did you call the police?"

Ethan shifted the shopping bag he was carrying to his left hand. "Yes," he said. "This . . . likely has nothing to do with that."

One of the newer stockboys whom Kerry barely knew

was gathering shopping carts. He looked over at the mention of police and asked, "You okay, Kerry?"

"Would you like a ride home?" Ethan asked before she could answer.

Kerry was aware of the stockboy watching and realized this probably looked like a pickup. She nodded vigorously to Ethan, then told the stockboy—Bill? Will?—"If my father does show up, could you tell him Ethan's given me a ride home?" Not that the name would mean anything to her father, but it *did* show that she wasn't going off with a stranger.

"Sure." The stockboy crashed two lines of carts together.

Ethan had hold of her arm and was guiding her out into the parking lot before it occurred to Kerry that Ethan didn't have a car. "Oh. I just remembered. We're not riding your bicycle, are we?"

Ethan laughed. "No, that's pretty well totaled. I decided to go all out and borrow my uncle's car."

After the fancy house, Kerry was amazed to see that the car was only a Skylark—the same as her father's, although blue instead of white, and considerably newer. *Ah, well,* Kerry thought, remembering that there had been three doors to the garage. Probably Ethan had left the Porsche and the Rolls at home.

Ethan opened the passenger door for her, then tossed her backpack and his bag of groceries in the back. *Classic Coke and potato chips,* she noted. She wondered what yesterday's vampire hunters would make of that.

"Your leg's a lot better," she said as he got into the car beside her.

He turned on the engine and pulled out of the parking space before answering, "It wasn't as bad as it looked."

Which was hard to believe.

But his color was definitely better. And he was using his right hand as though it didn't hurt. He finally had a jacket, a brown leather one. She couldn't make out any bandaging under his sleeve, but all in all she decided he was lucky he hadn't been forced to stay in the hospital overnight.

"What did the police have to say?" she asked him when it became apparent he wasn't going to volunteer information.

Ethan shrugged. "They seemed to buy my story."

"The others didn't contradict you?"

"No."

"The police arrested them? All of them?"

Ethan glanced at her. "Yes." As they passed through pools of brightness beneath some streetlights, his eyes seemed to flicker from light blue to black. "Why? What is it you're really asking?"

"It's just— I was afraid that all of this had something to do with my father not showing up."

"No," he said. He glanced at her again. "No. The police got them all: Daniel and Marcia Jordan, George Roth, Phil Sidowski."

It was strange to hear their full names. Not as reassuring as she would have thought, and strange.

He told her, "They won't be bothering you again."

"Are they going to jail?" Kerry asked.

He looked at her blankly.

"Or to a mental hospital?"

"That's for judges and lawyers to decide."

"But you'll have to testify?"

"Eventually. I suppose." He seemed to be getting annoyed with her questions. "I gave a full deposition to the police last night." Maybe that was it. He had volunteered to face them by himself, but maybe he resented it. Or maybe he was just exhausted. She was, and she had gone to bed about the time he was just beginning with the police.

"As for your father . . . ," Ethan said. "Your car is . . . old." He was too polite to call it a junk heap. But she had never been so aware of all its clunks and thuds and vibrations until riding in this newer and better-maintained version of the same model. "I'm sure he's sitting by the edge of the road, waiting for the triple A, even as we speak." He gave her a reassuring smile.

"I suppose," Kerry said. "The same thing happened with my mom once."

She said that because the previous night he had known Kerry's mother didn't live with them, and it seemed an opportunity to start a conversation; but he didn't ask for any details.

He was certainly less friendly and open than last night, more distant and self-assured. It was hard to put her finger on what it was that had originally made her think he was a freshman. *Had a falling out with Regina, did we?* she wondered.

It was just about 9:00 when they reached Fawn Meadow Circle. Most of the houses were brightly lit, and some even had Christmas decorations up, too, although this seemed premature to Kerry since it was only the first week of December and there was no snow. Amid all the lights, the Nowicki house looked not only totally dark but almost intimidating.

Ethan pulled up in front and gave her another reassuring smile.

"Thank you," Kerry said, reaching around the seat for her backpack.

"Anytime," Ethan assured her, but nothing was the same as last night.

Kerry got her key out of the pocket of the backpack and started up the walk, Ethan's headlights lighting her way.

Kerry put her hand on the doorknob, but before she even got the key in, the door swung open. Odd for her father not to lock up, but maybe he was at one of the neighbors' and had left thinking he'd only be away a few minutes; maybe he hadn't counted on being away after dark.

But that didn't fit in with the car being gone.

Kerry groped for the light switch.

The living room was a wreck.

Not *wreck* as in it-hadn't-been-cleaned-in-a-week. *Wreck* as in pictures askew, furniture tossed around, cushions slit.

Kerry whirled around just in time to see Ethan pulling away from the curb. "Wait!" she cried.

Ethan kept going.

Kerry dropped her backpack and raced across the lawn. "Ethan!" But it was winter; he had his windows rolled up. "Ethan!" She ran out into the street, waving her arms frantically. He was up to the corner stop sign, five houses away, and there was no way he could hear her and no way she could catch up. His brake lights were on, but in a second he'd go around the corner and she'd be on her own. What should she do? Go to the Armendarizes', she supposed. Or the Hagginses'; they were friendlier.

But Ethan's brake lights were still on. He must have seen her in his rearview mirror, for in a moment he began to back up. She ran down the street, reluctant to be near her house, afraid of whatever had happened in it.

Ethan rolled down his window.

"Somebody's broken in," Kerry said, panting. "We've been burglarized."

"Get in," Ethan told her.

He turned the car around and pulled up in front of the house. The light from the open door spilled brightly on the front stoop. No sign of movement. "Wait here," he told her. He left the car door open and didn't turn off the engine.

Kerry watched apprehensively as Ethan walked up the driveway. "Don't—," she whispered as he hesitated in the doorway, but then he stepped in and she lost sight of him. *Wait in the car*, where she couldn't see him? Alone? Right.

When she got to the house, Ethan hadn't moved beyond the living room. She had tried to be quiet, just in case the intruders were still in there, but when she saw what he was looking at—the red writing on the wall—she gasped.

Though he had his back to her, he must have heard her coming, because he wasn't startled. "It's just paint," he said. "It's just red paint."

"Are you sure?"

"Smell it."

The awful pain that had started in her chest loosened a bit. At least it wasn't blood.

VAMPIRE, the writing said, WE HAVE YOUR FAMILY.

CHAPTER SIX

"V AMPIRE?" KERRY SAID. "Somebody thinks I'm a *vampire?*"

There was additional writing below VAMPIRE, WE HAVE YOUR FAMILY. There were some letters and numbers that Kerry didn't understand at first and didn't take the time to try to work out: LEV 17:10.

"You said they got them." She turned on Ethan, who seemed unable to tear his gaze from the wall. "You said the police got all of them."

Quietly, sounding surprised more than concerned, Ethan said, "There must have been more than the four."

Kerry's voice became louder and shriller with each word:

"And with all their questioning, the police didn't figure that out?"

Ethan finally turned to face her.

"And the ones in custody," Kerry continued, "don't these others realize that they're making it worse for the ones who've already been arrested? We've got to call the police—"

Ethan was suddenly at her side, holding on to her elbow. She hadn't seen him move. She shrank back, startled, and he began pulling her to the door. "*Shh*," he warned.

"Ethan—"

He gave her a strong shake. His voice a whisper even after all her yelling, he said, "They might still be in the house."

That had been her first concern, but she'd forgotten in the horror of worrying about her father and Ian.

"We'll call from another phone," Ethan told her.

She nodded and let him lead her out of the house.

He closed the door behind them and picked up her backpack.

Kerry started to cut across the lawn to the Hagginses', but Ethan tugged on her arm in the direction of the car. "We've got to get to a phone," she insisted.

"If they're watching us," Ethan hissed at her, "that'll put us *and* your neighbors in danger." He hustled her to the car, tightening his grip when she tried to get one last look over her shoulder at the house windows.

"What if they're still in there?" she demanded. "My father and brother?"

"No." Ethan took off with a squeal of tires that in normal circumstances would have had her worried about Mrs. Armendariz. "They would have gotten them out of there first thing."

Why? Kerry was about to ask. *What makes you so sure?*

But before she had a chance, Ethan made a right-hand turn, going the direction opposite from his uncle's house, which was where she had assumed he was heading—and she said, "It'll be faster to call nine-one-one than to go all the way to the police station."

"If they suspect you're a vampire, it's because you helped me last night. They may well be watching my house. We'll call from Regina's."

"But—"

"Kerry!" he snapped in a tone that was equivalent to *Be quiet!*

She had been going to ask whether he was sure Regina would be home on a Friday night, but maybe he knew where she kept a spare key. He was obviously trying to work something out—who knew what?—and she gave him the benefit of the doubt. Her own mind, meanwhile, closed down and just went around and around a single thought: *I hope they're all right. Please, God, let them be all right.*

REGINA'S WAS A brick house surrounded by more-modern but still old wooden houses that stood on what had originally been all one property. There were lights on downstairs and in one of the upstairs windows, and Regina's red Ferrari was parked in the driveway.

Kerry opened her car door as soon as the car stopped, but she hesitated when Ethan made no move to turn off the engine or get out. He rested his elbows on the steering wheel, leaning forward, studying the house. "What?" she demanded.

"Something's wrong."

She wanted to call him paranoid, but the accusation died somewhere between intent and vocalization. She listened, because that seemed to be what he was doing. Then she lowered her voice to a whisper. "What do you hear?"

"Nothing." He said it as though it should be significant.

But it *was* December. The house windows were closed; the car windows were rolled up; and quiet as this car was compared to her father's, there was the engine noise.

In another moment he turned off the car and stepped outside. She stood next to him on the front walk. "She's home," she said as the upstairs light suddenly went off and the one in what had to be the next room went on.

"Automatic lights," Ethan told her.

After what felt like at least a half hour but was probably closer to ten or fifteen seconds, she demanded, "What are you listening for?"

He gave her a long look but didn't answer.

She wondered if he was going to tell her to wait outside, but when he finally went up to the front door, he didn't say anything, maybe waiting to see what she would choose on her own. She was about two steps behind him.

He had his own key; she told herself she wasn't surprised. It certainly made things easier.

"*Merde*," Ethan said the instant the door opened.

She'd had French in junior high, and though she remembered little else, she remembered the words Madame Welch had carefully but somewhat naïvely tried to steer them away from: "Well, yes, dear, that's almost right, but don't put a *d* in, or it's a vulgar expression." Kerry had a pretty good idea what Ethan had just said, but in the instant it took her to wonder why he'd said it—much less why he'd said it in French—he'd taken off across the living room and was going up the stairs two at a time.

In the well-lit downstairs Kerry caught a glimpse of

polished wood walls and expensive antiques. Everything was orderly, nothing obviously amiss—certainly nothing like what had happened at her house. But no matter how comfortable and secure it looked, she wasn't willing to get separated from Ethan, especially not with *something* having rattled him.

She ran up the stairs after him. He'd ignored the room with the light that they'd seen from the street, didn't glance left or right but made straight for the last room at the end of the hall. Kerry did it more slowly, half expecting someone to leap out at her.

The rooms—guest bedrooms, a workroom with computer and fax machine, a bathroom big enough to fit two of the Nowickis' bathrooms—were empty. But something *was* wrong. Surely it was more than jumpiness on Ethan's part.

He had taken several steps into what had to be the master bedroom, but he was just standing there. Unasked for came the memory of how he'd stood in much the same way at her house, staring at the message written on her wall. She came up behind him, sure he was aware of her despite the fact that he didn't turn around. He was still in that attitude of listening, of studying intently, though the room was dark. The light was on behind them, in the brass-and-oak bathroom.

Ethan was making no attempt to find the room light. Kerry remembered passing a switch that was probably for the hall light, but she hesitated. Surely he had seemed familiar enough with the layout of the house. Surely he and Regina were sleeping together; she should have no more delusions about that. He should know where the light in this room was.

So why was he standing in the dark?

In the seconds it took her to work that out, her eyes became accustomed enough to the dark that the last thing in the world she wanted was more light.

The easiest thing to make out was the big brass bed. Her first impression was that the covers were all lumpy and askew, that the bed wasn't made. But then she thought, no, there was someone in the bed. Except that the shape was all wrong. Not someone, but . . . Two dogs? A larger one stretched out in the middle and one of those hairy little dust-mop-looking ones on the pillow? But Regina didn't seem the kind of person who'd own dogs, much less let them sleep on her bed. And they weren't moving. Kerry was finding it hard to breathe, to hold back the growing conviction that it was, in fact, Regina in the bed. And that—if it was—the head was much too far removed from the body.

"Ethan?" she whispered, less in a voice than on the simple exhaling of a breath. She wanted to look away before her eyes became any more accustomed to the dark, but she couldn't.

He swore in French again. Several times.

The light went off in the bathroom—

Not in here, she prayed.

—and came on in the computer room across from the bathroom.

Which was still enough to show that the lumps were definitely Regina.

Kerry finally managed a backward step. "Who would do such a thing?" she asked.

"Vampire hunters," Ethan whispered.

He's in shock, she thought. *He's saying it, but it hasn't sunk in yet.* Which had to be a mercy.

He was saying, still never looking at her, "That's one way humans kill vampires: expose them to sunlight, then chop off the head and stuff the mouth with garlic. I've never been clear what the garlic's supposed to do."

Kerry remembered the awful stillness in her own house. They had never checked those bedrooms. *Not Dad,* she thought. *Not Ian.* Nobody could think that of Ian. She couldn't stop shaking. *"They make 'em when they're still kids?"* Roth had asked. This was all her fault. She should have gone to the police herself.

She headed for the computer room, found the phone, dialed: 9–1—

Ethan set his hand down to disconnect her call.

"If there's someone here," she pointed out, "they'd certainly have heard us, they'd have had the chance to come out and get us."

"Just wait—," Ethan started, but she pulled the phone away from him.

"For what this time?"

His eyes, that lovely shade of blue, scanned her face. Looking for what?

"Kerry . . ."

She was willing to forgive bad choices. But too many things were beginning to sink in. Like the way he'd run up the stairs with no trace of a limp. Like how there was no evidence of that awful bruise he'd had on his temple last night.

He reached to take the phone from her, and she yanked back on the sleeve of his jacket, exposing a pale and perfectly unmarred wrist where yesterday she'd cut him so badly she had been sure he'd need stitches.

After all she'd seen, and despite all logic, she couldn't be surprised. "You're exactly what they said," she told him, less question than statement. "You're a vampire."

Lest she have any lingering doubts, he took the phone from her and yanked the cord out of the wall.

CHAPTER SEVEN

SOMEHOW, BEFORE KERRY was aware of Ethan moving, he'd tossed the phone aside and had taken hold of her wrist. The coldness of his skin seeped into hers. How had she never noticed that before?

She tried to squirm away, but though he wasn't holding tight enough to hurt, she couldn't budge.

He caught up her other wrist and drew her in closer. "I'm not going to hurt you," he told her.

She tried to knee him in the groin, which always seemed to work in the movies, but he was too fast for her, and in a moment he had her backed up against the wall.

"Don't," she whispered.

Still holding her wrists up against the wall, he took half

a step back so that he wasn't pressed against her. It wasn't much of a gamble on his part—not with that speed and strength. And she didn't have enough room to struggle anyway. But at the very least he was inconveniencing himself, and for no other reason that she could see than to make a declaration that he wasn't going to take advantage of the situation.

She was angry at the relief that weakened her knees, that made her want to look at him more favorably just because he wasn't thoroughly despicable.

"I'm sorry," he told her. She fought not to read sincerity into his voice. She knew he was a liar. Everything he'd said so far had been a lie. "You're involved in this purely by accident, and for whatever it's worth, I swear to you I *am* grateful for last night . . . and I never thought to see you again."

Her eyes were hot and stinging. She fought to keep them open—to face what was coming—and not to cry. It would have been easier but for the strand of hair that had gotten loose and was poking at the edge of her eye.

"I'll do all in my power to save your father and your brother," he told her. No doubt to keep her calm until it was too late. He shifted position so that he held both her hands in his left, and he used his free hand to brush the hair out of her face.

She cringed from his touch.

"I'm not going to hurt you," he repeated.

She forced herself to look directly into his eyes. "Does that mean you're not going to harm me, or does it mean that when you kill me, it's not going to hurt?"

He didn't answer, which was answer enough.

There was no malice in his blue eyes. Maybe he was sorry,

as he said; he certainly was being as gentle as he could, but she saw his gaze flick briefly to her throat. He slipped his right hand behind her neck, supporting her head, and pulled her in closer so she was pressed against his chest.

"Wait," she said, "please." Her own struggles brought them into more intimate contact than he'd attempted on his own, and she shrank back in panic. "Don't," she begged, knowing that surely she was trying his patience, that his kindness would stretch just so far, that if he were truly kind he could never have survived as a vampire. "Listen, please." She stopped struggling, to show she wasn't just stalling for time. Not that she could stop shaking or gasping for breath. "Just a minute. Just listen for one minute."

He hadn't bitten her yet. For this moment at least he was only holding her steady, and she forced herself not to think about their relative positions. She felt his breath, light on her throat, which was unexpected. She realized she'd been feeling his heartbeat, too, a steady five or six beats a minute, belying the coldness of his touch.

"I can help you," she told him, determined to make herself useful to him, determined to make her family valuable to him.

His eyes searched her face, as though he honestly wanted to find something there to make himself believe her. "Oh, Kerry," he said, soft as a sigh.

"You want to find the vampire hunters who killed Regina, don't you?" she cried as he bent over her throat again. He hesitated, looking up at her through a fringe of dark hair. "You want to find who killed her before any of the other vampires start getting killed, don't you?" It was a risk. Regina could have been a hapless mortal like Kerry herself, assumed guilty by the vampire hunters because of her association with

Ethan. Her death could mean nothing to him. If so, Kerry didn't have anything else to offer. But she didn't think so. If nothing else, there was the matter of how dark it had been in Regina's room. Inner shutters as well as drapes, she was willing to bet.

In any case, Ethan had his head raised. He was watching her, waiting.

"They think I'm one of you," she continued, putting it together in her mind even as the words came out. "But they're hoping to draw me out of hiding by using my family. Maybe you can draw *them* out by using *me*."

At least he was considering it.

"I have nothing to lose," she said, remembering, a moment later, that he had said the same thing last night. It couldn't hurt to remind him he owed her his life . . . or rather, his continued existence. "At least this way I get a chance. My dad and Ian get a chance. I can go places you can't. Or at least, I can go at times you can't. It'd be like gaining back the daylight."

His expression told her nothing. She should probably be mentally preparing herself for death—that would be more useful than pleading. But how *did* one prepare for death? And while she was trying to work that one out, he stepped back. Then he released her arms and stepped back farther. With a slight smile he bowed his head to indicate acceptance. For the moment.

She still couldn't see that his teeth were long enough to have done what he had been about to do. But she had no doubt how close she'd come to dying. It was hard to get her voice to work, but she asked, "What assurance do I have that if I help you in good faith, you'll let me and my family live afterward?"

Ethan looked surprised, then he laughed, seeming genuinely amused. "None."

She realized that, like Regina's, his ready smile was most often pretense. She supposed that after a couple hundred years vampires had probably heard everything, seen everything, done everything already; no doubt most of the time they were bored out of their minds. She wondered—same old question, but with a new twist—how old Ethan really was. Old enough to have developed acting skills, definitely. And to be a good judge of people. He had seen that she would respond well to a poor frightened victim, so that was what he had been for her when he needed her help last night. No doubt he could convincingly be other things for other people.

In a moment all trace of humor was completely gone from his face. His voice was neither harsh nor threatening; he might have been reading course descriptions from the college catalog: "Of course, if I even suspect the possibility of betrayal, your family will be the ones to pay for it." His voice got even softer. "Believe this, Kerry: An easy death is only one of the choices I can offer."

He waited to see that she believed, which she most emphatically did. Then, "Come," he said, putting his hand out for her.

She took one step forward, to show that she would follow and he didn't need to hold on to her. He didn't move, so they stood face-to-face looking at each other until she finally gave him her hand. She shivered as his cold, strong fingers closed around hers. *How are vampires made?* she wondered. *Had a vampire bitten him when he'd still been mortal? Human,* she corrected herself. He'd referred to nonvampires as *human,* as though humans and vampires were two different species. Which

74

probably made killing people easier. The stories she'd read and movies she'd seen offered conflicting methods. Surely there was more to it than a vampire's victims becoming vampires; after enough years of that, there'd be more vampires than humans. Or was there something about being bitten a certain number of times? And what about being buried in unconsecrated ground? Kerry wondered if Ethan had spent any time in a grave. The thought made her shiver. But he only led her as far as the desk, and if he noticed—he didn't comment.

Ethan sat down and turned on the computer; it made the distinctive high-pitched squeals that indicated it was attached to a modem. He watched her while he waited for the screen to come up, probably to see how quickly she caught on to what he was doing. It took a couple seconds. *Fast, slow, or average?* she wondered, sure that he could tell from her face the moment she guessed, though she couldn't tell anything from his face. And she doubted she could have even in better light than from the flickering monitor.

Once the prompt appeared, he typed, one-handed because he was still holding onto her hand: "Had to leave abruptly. Regina can't come. I'll catch up when I can. Michael."

"Is that your real name?" Kerry asked, trying to decide whether he looked more like a Michael or an Ethan.

He looked in her direction but didn't answer, and in the dim light she still couldn't make out his expression, if he had any.

"You're warning the other vampires, aren't you?" she asked. "What is this, a bulletin board for vampires? You all subscribe to the service and every day—every night—you check for secret messages to see if anybody's on your trail?"

"Something like that," Ethan acknowledged.

"I thought the big advantage of being a vampire was living forever, not having to be afraid of anything."

Ethan didn't answer. He stood, and this time he headed downstairs. They made their way without turning on any lights. Part of that could be thorough familiarity with the house, but Kerry was beginning to suspect that Ethan could see in the dark a lot better than she could, especially after he skirted a kitchen table that Kerry didn't see till she collided with it.

He paused long enough to let her rub her bruised hip.

"Are there other vampires in Brockport you need to warn?" Kerry asked.

"Oh yeah." Ethan's sarcasm was thick enough to recognize without seeing the smirk on his face. "Brockport, New York, is a regular hotbed of vampire activity."

She put that down as something to remember. It might prove useful at a later date: that Ethan and Regina could well be the only vampires in the area. Or was that just what he wanted her to think? "So, what were you and Regina doing here?" she asked.

He was back to not answering.

"What about Rochester?" she continued. "Any vampires there? Or in Buffalo?"

He pulled her around to look directly at her. She could barely make him out in the soft glow that was all that reached them from the light now on in the living room. "Don't," he warned in a soft and matter-of-fact voice, "make a nuisance of yourself."

"Sorry," she said. "I don't know what I need to know to keep both of us alive." Not that Ethan was, strictly speaking, alive.

76

"You don't need to know about other vampires," Ethan told her.

"Right," she said. And then again—because it couldn't hurt, "Sorry."

Vampires in Rochester and Buffalo, she noted mentally.

Ethan opened a door that could have led directly into a blank wall for all she could make out in the dark. But he took a step down; she could feel that. "I can't see a thing," she said. "If you've got the extra energy to keep me from tumbling down the basement stairs, that's fine, but wouldn't it be easier on both of us if you just turned the light on?" She hoped she sounded as brave as she thought she did.

He stepped back onto the same level and reached behind her. The light over the basement stairs came on. "Better?" he asked.

"Yes." Politeness couldn't hurt. Even if it wasn't sincere. "Thank you." Not that she liked the idea of going down there with him. *What can he do to me down there,* she tried to console herself, *that he couldn't have done just as well upstairs?*

Besides bury my body when he's through?

But Ethan said, "Sometimes I forget," by which she took him to mean sometimes he forgot human limitations, which was probably as close to an apology as she'd get from him. Just when she'd worked that out he added, "Don't become a smart aleck."

He tugged on her arm, the only warning she got before their hasty descent of the stairs.

The idea of burying didn't seem so clever when Kerry saw that the basement had a dirt floor. Were any of Regina's victims down here? she wondered. Was Ethan planning on burying Regina?

The place was a mess. It looked as though Regina had

gone through at least two sets of furniture for every room and piled all the extras down here. Among all the other stuff, Kerry spied a moped, practically furry with dust. That seemed to be what Ethan was heading for. But he stopped just short of it, picking up instead a red-and-yellow can that sloshed when he shook it. *Gasoline,* Kerry's father would say, *belongs in a garage or shed; it's dangerous in a house.*

And where's Dad now? she wondered.

"You're not going to—," she started.

He did. He poured great dollops of gasoline on a green damask love seat with tassels.

"But what about the neighbors?" she demanded, not quite having the courage to grab his arm. She couldn't have made him stop in any case, but she felt guilty for not making the attempt. It was a five-gallon drum, and it had sounded just about full. "What if the fire spreads?"

"Not likely, with a brick exterior," Ethan said. "And it's necessary in any case. I have no idea what she has here, what people could find. Old pictures, papers. Seeming anachronisms that might get someone thinking."

It was how vampires survived, Kerry realized: people not thinking about vampires anymore, not believing, seeking rational explanations. Like assuming that vampire hunters were crazies. No wonder he was jumpy at the idea of a big old houseful of proof. He still had hold of her hand, and he pulled her along as he kept on pouring gasoline all the way up the cellar stairs, across the kitchen, into the living room, and up the stairs to the second level. The automatic light had come on in the guest bedroom closest to Regina's room. Kerry balked, but he dragged her along as effortlessly as a child with a pull toy.

He pulled her into the room, carefully set down the gasoline can, then shoved her against the tall antique armoire on the wall opposite from the bed. "Little girls who hang around with vampires need to get used to dead things," he said, blocking her escape by leaning against the armoire with an arm outstretched on either side of her. "In fact, little girls who hang around with vampires already are with dead things."

Kerry had no idea how to handle the sudden fierceness in his voice. "I'm sorry Regina is dead," she said, thinking that might be it. Or that the acknowledgment of his possible grief might make up for her earlier mouthiness.

"Regina," Ethan said, "has been dead—" But he cut off whatever he had been going to say, evidently deciding that was something else about vampires she didn't need to know. ". . . for a long time," he finished with a blatantly insincere smile. "And I very much doubt any living soul is sorry."

He shoved her toward the bed. The sight wasn't as bad—and it was worse—than she'd anticipated. There was the hair, which Kerry recognized, but the body looked the way she imagined an unwrapped mummy might look: charred, blackened, and withered, more like a hairless monkey than anything human. Even the nightgown Regina had been wearing and the sheets beneath her were scorched. Kerry glanced at the windows.

"Obviously opened at some point during the day," Ethan said vehemently. "Then reclosed to look normal."

"What do you want me to do?" she asked, which—while not a safe course—was the least-likely-to-provoke-him thing she could think of to say.

"Open all the windows," Ethan replied, returning to his customary bland tone.

"Fine," she told him. She had been afraid he'd want her closer to—perhaps even touching—that thing on the bed that had been Regina.

There were shutters. She'd guessed right. She flung them open and raised the windows, all the while aware of Ethan behind her, pulling loose all the sheets and bedcoverings, and wrapping up Regina's body. "Get the other windows on this floor," he ordered.

She considered making a break for it, but if his hearing was as good as his eyesight, he'd know before she made it past the first step. She remembered how he'd stood in front of the house listening and had known something was wrong. *"What do you hear?"* she'd asked. *"Nothing,"* he'd answered. Was it that he couldn't hear Regina's heartbeat? Her once-every-ten-or-fifteen-seconds heartbeat? And once they entered the house . . . Kerry shuddered. He'd started swearing as soon as he opened the door, and he'd gone right to Regina. It could only have been the scent of her spilled blood.

There was no use trying to run.

Kerry had gotten five windows in three rooms open when Ethan called her. "I'm not—," she started.

"That's all right."

She figured he knew exactly which windows she'd opened, and how hard she'd exerted herself for each one. She'd never before been so conscious of her heart pounding in her chest, her blood flowing through her veins.

From the doorway, Kerry saw that Ethan had Regina and her bedding on the floor, rolled up in a quilt that he'd gotten from the quilt rack at the foot of the bed. From the smell of gasoline, she realized he'd doused the mattress.

As soon as Kerry walked in, he struck a match and tossed

it onto the bed. The fire started with a great *whoosh,* faster than she'd have imagined.

Her inclination was to run immediately, but Ethan handed her the matches. "Three more," he told her. "The first down the basement stairs, the second in the living room, and the third tossed up the stairs right before you leave."

"Me?" Her voice came out as a squeak. It was hard to concentrate with the room so hot already and the overpowering smell of the gasoline. The book of matches sat in her hand, strangely heavy and incongruous. It was obviously a wedding favor—silver bells on a white background, with the message "Steve and Beth, May 24, 1947."

"The first down the basement stairs," Ethan repeated, "the second—"

"—in the living room," she finished, "and the third on the stairs." He was keeping her alive to help him; if she didn't start helping soon, he was bound to reconsider.

"Very good," he told her.

As she ran out of the already smoky room, she was aware of him picking up Regina's body easily and flinging it over his shoulder. He was only a step behind when she veered off toward the kitchen. She lit a match, thinking only at the last instant to make sure she wasn't standing in a puddle of gasoline before she dropped it.

She lit the second match in the living room, but her hands were shaking too hard to get the third going. The smoke was stinging her eyes, her throat felt as though she'd been drinking gasoline, and she thought, *If he wants a third, he can do it himself.*

Ethan was already sitting in the car, the engine going, when she slammed Regina's front door behind her.

She could scream. She probably would have time for one *Fire!* or *Vampire!* or *Help!*

But only one.

She got into the car, very much aware of the bundle in the backseat, the decapitated body of a murdered vampire. Very much aware of the living—more or less—vampire beside her.

And very much aware, before they reached the end of the street, of the dark smoke filling the darker sky behind them.

CHAPTER EIGHT

AFTER SEVERAL MINUTES of driving, Kerry roused herself enough to ask, "Where are we going?"

"Bergen Swamp," Ethan answered.

"There's a swamp in Bergen?" The Bergen town line was about two minutes from Main Street, Brockport. "I thought Bergen was mostly farms and student housing."

Ethan glanced at her. "Well, it's hardly in the same category as the Florida Everglades. But, yeah, it's a swampy, wooded area. Good for hunting."

For a moment Kerry thought he meant vampires hunted people there. Then she realized he meant game hunters, after deer and rabbits. "Oh." She was unable to hide the relief in her voice.

He glanced at her again, and again what she was thinking must have been transparent. He sighed, loudly, and shook his head.

Kerry looked around at the familiar countryside rolling by in the darkness: fields and occasional houses. Her heart did a quick flutter, but she tried to keep her voice casual. "I hate to be the one to break the news to you, but you passed through Bergen about five minutes ago."

He gave her one of those looks she was beginning to think of as a vampire-thinks-of-amusing-thought-that-is-amusing-only-to-other-vampires look. "I thought we were talking about long-term goals," he said. "We have a couple errands to run on the way."

"Such as?"

"You aren't going to like them, so I'd rather put off telling you." He saw her expression and laughed. "But I doubt they're as bad as what you're thinking."

What she was thinking was that they were heading off toward Rochester to find a victim for him to feed on. The awful, frustrating thing was that—even if that should turn out to be what he intended—when the time came, chances were there would be absolutely nothing she could do to prevent it.

She forced herself to think of alternatives. Maybe he was telling the truth. For once. They were definitely going in the direction of Rochester, and there was little else between here and there except towns even smaller than Brockport.

Rochester. It suddenly came to her. He was going to enlist the help of other vampires. Which probably significantly increased her chances of losing her own blood.

He was watching her, evaluating, still amused. "Besides," he added, "we have time to kill."

And she was sure he was aware she could think of two ways to take that. She intentionally ignored one of them.

"What about my family?" she demanded. "Aren't you forgetting them?"

"Definitely not," he answered brightly. "They're absolutely the only control I have over you."

It wasn't exactly the answer she'd anticipated. "Well?"

"*Well* what?"

"They're in danger. Now, unless you know that they're being held captive in Rochester—and I don't see how you could know that unless—" She stopped. *Was* Ethan involved? Had he arranged for Ian and her dad to be kidnapped as part of some elaborate vampire scheme to . . . But she couldn't work it out in any way that made sense at all.

Beside her, Ethan waited patiently for her to continue.

"Unless you know that they're being held captive in Rochester, we seem to be headed away from them."

"I have no idea where they're being held," he told her. "Was that what you were asking?"

"I was asking . . . I was pointing out, because of the time involved . . . Couldn't you do whatever it is you're going to do with a phone call?"

Ethan gave her a puzzled look and said, "No," in a tone strongly indicating she was wrong about the purpose of this trip being to communicate with Rochester vampires.

She said, "What if whoever has Dad and Ian . . ." She needed a deep breath to continue. ". . . kills them while we're busy running your errands?"

"Kerry, I don't know who has your family. But if they're still alive—now, at this moment—it doesn't make sense for whoever has them to kill them. They're useless dead."

"Unless I don't know they're dead."

"There is that," he acknowledged. "But there was nobody at your house. I would have heard. And I would have known"—he was saying this last part slowly, phrasing it carefully—"if your father and your brother were dead in the house. If there had been a quantity of spilled blood, I would have known it."

Kerry spared a thought to be pleased that she had been right about that. And if she could keep her wits about her, gather enough useful information, she just might be able to overcome Ethan, rescue Dad and Ian, and come out of this alive.

Ethan was saying, "So they probably weren't dead at the house and it would be no advantage to take them away from the house and *then* kill them. Whoever is after me has invested a significant amount of time studying the situation. He . . . She . . . They . . . aren't going to rush things now. I'd say your family is safe enough for the next few days. Their best hope is for us not to become overly hasty through misplaced concern."

Kerry tried to find the flaws in his reasoning, besides the obvious one: that he had no concern for her family. "That works out well for you," she finally said.

He just flashed a cold smile.

When he didn't volunteer any more information, she asked, "What are we going to do at the Bergen Swamp once we get there?"

Ethan stopped for a red light out in the middle of a country crossroad, no other traffic in sight. He rested his face in his hands. "Get rid of Regina's body."

Kerry still hadn't been able to figure out what he felt about Regina's death: grief for a loved one, or annoyance because the circumstances were inconvenient, or something else she couldn't begin to guess. Every time she settled on one, he did or said something that shifted the balance again. *Could* vampires love?

"The light's changed," she told him.

After a few more miles of silence she asked, "So she's truly dead?"

This time he couldn't seem to grasp what she was asking.

Before he was forced to state the obvious, that her head had been cut off, Kerry said, "I mean, I thought the only way to kill a vampire was a stake through the heart."

He was looking at her as though she were crazy. The worst part was she wasn't sure why.

"I thought anything less than that, the vampire would recover from."

Though for the moment they still seemed centered in the correct lane, he hadn't glanced away from her to check the road for what seemed to be an incredibly long stretch.

"Like you recovered from your injuries," she said. "Would you please watch the road?"

"God," he said.

Excuse me for my ignorance, she wanted to say. *I wasn't exactly sure what the term* undead *covered.* Instead, she just said, "Well, I didn't know."

"What, you thought her head would grow a new body? Or her body a new head? Or the two pieces could just be stuck together, like—"

"All right, I'm sorry. I thought *your* recovery was just about miraculous."

"It wasn't anywhere near the same," he snapped.

"All right."

He cast a sudden worried look at her, which came a moment before she realized she had learned a potentially valuable lesson: Vampires were susceptible to a variety of deaths, if the injuries were severe enough.

She said, "All I was asking was if she'd be coming back."

"She won't be coming back," Ethan said. There was no way to tell how much he suspected she guessed.

IT WAS ABOUT a forty-five-minute drive to Rochester. Kerry asked herself about forty-five times if she was doing the right thing. How far should she trust Ethan? That was an easy one: not at all. And yet—and yet—he had let her live, when all he had needed her for so far was to light the gasoline while he carried Regina's body to the car. With an extra two minutes he could have done that himself. Yet why bring her to Rochester to kill her when he could have done it at Regina's house? Unless he didn't want her charred bones found in the wreckage of the house, for some reason she couldn't work out. Or unless there were some sort of vampire hierarchy, and he planned to offer her as a gift to the chief or king or president vampire. Which didn't make a whole lot of sense.

As they reached the suburbs, as they slowed from the fifty-five m.p.h. speed limit and started having to stop for lights and traffic, Kerry wondered what were her chances of surviving should she throw herself out of the car and run screaming for help. Not very good, she estimated. Surely Ethan had taken into consideration that she *might* try something of that nature. No doubt he had confidence in his ability to stop her before she attracted attention. But he was still taking a risk. What could he possibly hope to gain?

Unless he had spoken the truth. Unless he needed her help to get to Regina's killers.

If that was the case, escaping—even if possible—would doom Dad and Ian.

But how likely was it Ethan would let her live with all that she was seeing and learning about vampires? Which brought her right back to: Was she doing the right thing?

Kerry had been hoping that whatever Ethan needed he could find in one of the outlying suburbs, but he drove right into the city. Not only that, but into one of the sleazier parts of the city.

"Do you trust me?" Ethan asked.

"No." Kerry was amazed that he even had to ask.

He gave his soft, pleasant, insincere laugh. "All for the best, I suppose, but that's going to make this more difficult. Please don't do anything stupid."

He'd been looking for a parking space and now he pulled over. Even though it was eleven o'clock, this particular section of the city was brightly lit; at least those buildings that weren't boarded over and spray-painted were brightly, even garishly, lit. Women—and some girls who looked not quite as old as Kerry herself—walked by in tight skirts and high heels. Despite the cold, most had their jackets unbuttoned or unzipped so they could be seen better. The jacket of choice seemed to be rabbit with leather trim. There were a few young men, too, though most of the men were in the cars that very slowly cruised down the street.

"What are we doing here?" Kerry demanded.

"Shopping."

She'd been right the first time. He was looking for someone to drain of blood, someone who wouldn't be missed.

Ethan tugged on her arm, trying to get her to come out the driver's door, obviously suspecting that if he got out first she might lock the doors behind him, which at the moment struck her as a very good idea. Kerry clutched the door handle and dug in with her sneakers and her bottom.

Ethan pulled, strongly enough to make her slide effort-lessly across the seats. "I asked you not to do anything stupid," he hissed into her ear.

Out on the street, the prostitutes watched with mild in-terest. She was sure they thought she was one of them and they were wondering if he was through with her and going to trade her in. Even when it was apparent he wasn't going to let go of her arm, some of the women blew kisses or stood with their hands in their pockets, holding their jackets open, just in case.

She was concentrating so much on the people around them, she didn't realize until the last second that Ethan was leading her into one of the stores. She balked when she saw the sign:

LOVE, ETC.
books, videos, etc.

"Trust me," Ethan whispered, beyond all reason. "It's not as bad as you think."

The store was awful. Lingerie with cutouts. Men's bikini briefs with peacock feathers. Posters of couples: men and women, men and men, women and women. There was no place Kerry could look that she didn't see something em-barrassing. And she felt stupid because some of the stuff was embarrassing even though she didn't know what it was. And then she felt stupid to feel stupid, because there was no reason for *her* to feel embarrassed. The people who ran the store should be embarrassed.

At least Ethan kept a tight hold on her hand while he spoke to the man behind the counter. Her hand was sweaty; his, as always, was colder than any living person's. For the moment she didn't mind what they looked like. She *wanted*

people to think they were together. Especially the other customer in the store, a scuzzy-looking man in a long coat. Kerry
stared at her feet, sure that if she glanced up he was going
to flash her.

She suddenly realized that what Ethan was buying were
handcuffs. Which was bad, but probably not as bad as it
could be. If he wanted to restrain her physically, he was strong
enough to do it without handcuffs.

"Enjoy," the clerk said with a smirk in his voice.

Back at the car, they got in the same way they'd gotten
out, through the driver's side. Once settled, Ethan turned to
her and asked, "Are you all right?"

As if he couldn't see that she was shaking. "Fine," she
snapped. "How not?"

"If I intended you harm . . . ," he said with his mocking
smile. "Well, I wouldn't need these. These are protection."

So they were for her.

What was he waiting for? For her to acknowledge that
he was doing her a favor?

"Compared to this," Ethan said as he started the engine
and pulled away from the curb, "the next part will be a piece
of cake."

After a while she couldn't take it anymore. "What's the
next part?" she asked.

"We steal a car."

CHAPTER NINE

THEY PULLED INTO a car dealership on the outskirts of Rochester. The place was closed, but the parking lot was well lit. No doubt to keep people from doing exactly what Ethan was planning on doing.

"We already have a car," Kerry said miserably. "Why do you need another one?"

"I don't want this one noticed anywhere near the Bergen Swamp."

What was worse was knowing he was right. Every step of the way, he kept making decisions that were right, and she kept getting pulled further and further into the wrong. What would Dad say if he knew what she was doing? Dad had made her take a ring she'd found on the running track at school to campus security—that was how honest he was. How would he react to her stealing a car? *Let me find out,* she prayed. She was willing to face anything if she could only know that she'd find Dad and Ian alive on the other side of it.

Ethan made her get out in front of the big door marked SERVICE DEPT.

"You should turn off the headlights, shouldn't you?" she suggested. "So we'll be less obvious?"

"I want to be obvious. Here, lean on the hood, pretend to fill this out." He handed her a form he'd gotten from a metal container by the door.

"What are we doing?" she asked as he reached under the driver's seat and pulled out a flannel-wrapped package about the size of an envelope but a little thicker. "And what's that?"

"*These* are various-size lock picks. And *we* are using the overnight drop-off service, in case the police drive by."

Kerry leaned on the hood and stared at the form. Ethan was looking into the parked cars. "If these cars are broken and need to be fixed," she asked, "how do we know the one we'll take won't have its engine fall out halfway there?"

"Well, of course we can't be sure," Ethan replied as he crouched down on the far side of a blue Shadow, presumably to fiddle with the lock, "though I do believe the manufacturer generally prefers the term *serviced* to *fixed.* And I don't think a car is ever technically referred to as *broken.*"

"Whatever," Kerry grumbled.

He opened the door, and his voice became muffled as he leaned to do something with the steering column. "In this particular case, the car has just over a thousand miles, so it probably isn't *broken* at all; it's in for its thousand-mile warranty check. And—special bonus at no extra cost—it's blue."

"Don't tell me, blue is your favorite color." The Skylark was blue, too, though a darker shade.

"Blue is a wonderfully nondescript color for a car," Ethan said. "Nobody notices a blue car." The Shadow's engine rumbled to life.

"Handy trick," Kerry said. "Where did you learn so much about cars?"

"Ah, it's something they teach us in vampire school." Before she could think of a suitable reply, Ethan had stashed his breaking-and-entry tools in his pocket. "Get in," he told her.

While she did, he doused the lights on the Skylark and transferred Regina's quilt-wrapped body to the backseat of the Shadow. He'd also gotten the denim jacket from Regina's car, probably while Kerry was busy torching Regina's house.

"Leftovers?" she asked as Ethan tossed it into the Shadow's backseat. "From one of Regina's victims?"

"Possibly." Ethan shrugged. "I certainly didn't know all of Regina's business. It's history now."

At least that's over, she thought once the evidence was safely in the new car. But the instant he slammed the back door, Kerry saw a black-and-white police car turn into the parking lot. *I'm going to get killed,* she thought. *Either Ethan's going to rip my throat out so I can't tell them anything, or we'll crash and burn during a high-speed chase, or the police will open fire. . . .*

But far from seeming perturbed, Ethan walked slowly around the front of their newly acquired car to the passenger side, where he rapped his knuckles on her window.

Incredulous, she rolled it down.

"Do you have the form?" he asked.

"I didn't really fill it out," she whispered.

"I should hope not." He took it from her and stood there

as though checking what she'd written then he dropped it into the mail-slot-like opening in the service department's door.

The police car was cruising the lot, shining a light in the salesroom.

Still not hurrying, Ethan got into the car beside her. "How about stopping for an ice cream?" he asked.

"You're not taking this seriously enough," she told him, even though the police showed no inclination thus far to arrest them or to open fire.

"But I am. We still have too much time. I don't want to go to the swamp until as late as possible, to lessen our chances of being seen." Ethan pulled out of the parking lot. "Don't look back," he warned. "I'm watching." After a few moments, he said, "They're not following us."

Kerry put her hands over her face. "I can't stand this."

"Nonsense," he told her. "You're a natural."

Which was not an encouraging thought.

"Why are we headed back toward Rochester?" Kerry asked.

"More traffic this way, just in case we *were* followed. Besides, I promised you ice cream."

"This is *not* a date."

He just laughed.

They stopped at a restaurant, where he insisted on buying her a sundae. After looking at the menu as though unable to make up his own mind, he finally told the waitress, "I'll just have a decaf." He smiled charmingly.

"Afraid of staying up all night?" Kerry asked.

He turned the smile on her. "Tell me about school," he said instead of answering.

"Why?"

"What else are we going to talk about in here? What electives are you taking? What do you hope for out of life?"

"Oh no." She set down her glass of water so firmly the water sloshed over the rim and onto her hand. "I'm not going to have you sit there and judge me and decide if my life is worthwhile."

"All right, then," he said equably. "Have you seen any good movies lately?"

She glared at him warily, wondering why he wanted to know, how he could possibly use this information against her.

The sundae came and once she smelled the hot fudge, she found that beyond all reason she was hungry after all. *How can I be hungry when I don't even know if my family is still alive?* she chided herself. *When I don't know whether I'll still be alive by the end of the night?* But it seemed silly to go hungry until then, just to spite Ethan.

Meanwhile, Ethan carried the conversation by himself, chattering about movies and TV and books and current events. He poured sugar and cream in his coffee, occasionally ran his finger around the rim or otherwise played with it but never drank a sip.

"Can we go?" she finally asked, as a group of bizarrely dressed young people came in, loud and laughing and obviously regulars.

"It's the *Rocky Horror Picture Show* contingent," Ethan said brightly. It was a relief for Kerry to learn they were apparently in costume and didn't normally dress that way, considering the makeup that some of them were wearing, boys as well as girls. Two or three had toilet paper draped over their shoulders. It wasn't a relief that a couple of them waved and Ethan waved back.

"Friends of yours?" she asked.

"Not the way you mean," he answered. "Have you ever been . . ." He let the question drift off and gave her one of those evaluating looks. "No, I don't suppose you have. You really should consider having some fun once in a while."

"How dare you—"

But at least he was getting up, paying, leaving.

She followed, scowling at the group of teenagers, unable to think of any way to warn them away from Ethan.

Outside, it was even colder than she had remembered, and her breath came out frostily. Apparently by this time Ethan had enough confidence that she wouldn't lock him out that he let her get in the car in the normal way. He even held the door for her. Then again, she remembered, he had his lock picks in his pocket.

"Geez, Kerry," he said, still in his just-an-average-guy-out-on-a-date mode, "you've really got to develop your conversational skills."

Of all the nerve. "If you talked about something important—," she started.

"We can talk about important things now that we're alone," he said, starting the car. "What shall we discuss?"

"The possibility of Regina's body getting blood all over the backseat of this car."

From infuriatingly cheerful, Ethan went straight into angry. "First of all," he said, "so what? Second, dead bodies don't bleed: it's the beating of the heart that causes blood to move through veins and arteries." Considering the way he generally kept his voice soft and even and unemotional, she was stunned by his vehemence, though she had no idea what he was so vehement about. "And third, there's no blood left in Regina's body anyway."

"What are you saying?" she asked. Suddenly the ice cream

sundae seemed to collect in the pit of her stomach like a solid lump. "You drank from her?" she whispered.

"No." Ethan gave her a look that indicated he was as horrified as she. "No," he repeated.

"Vampires can't drink each other's blood?" she asked.

"Of course they can drink each other's blood," he said. "How do you think—" He cut himself off. "But she was dead. That'd be like . . ."

"Never mind," she told him. By the look on his face, she didn't want to hear whatever analogy he came up with.

"It would be worse than drinking an animal's blood."

"Vampires don't drink animal blood?"

He shook his head.

She guessed: "Or . . . collected blood from the Red Cross?"

If the idea of drinking someone's blood did awful things to her stomach, apparently the suggestions she was making were doing the same things to his.

He pulled off the side of the road. Alarmed, Kerry backed up against the door, but he put his hands out in a conciliatory gesture. "I only want to explain," he said. "It's important you understand." He paused as though trying to organize his thoughts. Obviously this was something vampires didn't need to discuss between themselves, and just as obviously it wasn't something they normally shared with humans. Ethan was speaking hesitantly, having a hard time putting this into words. "It's not just the nourishment from the blood itself. There's . . ." He ran his hands through his hair, a nervous gesture she hadn't seen from him before. As though he realized what he was doing and wanted to hide this sign of strain, he rested his elbows on the steering wheel, not looking directly at her anymore, except to steal quick glances. He had his hands together, the fingers steepled, which almost looked like praying. Perhaps he had the same thought, for he shifted position, clasping his fingers together. "There's a physical and mental bond, a sharing of . . . the *spirit*, for lack of a better word. . . ."

Kerry took in a deep breath. "I think I've heard this line from the boy who took me to the harvest dance."

Ethan laughed with what sounded like genuine amusement, which was disconcerting because she hadn't meant to be funny. "There *is* a similarity." He looked at her appraisingly, as though trying to gauge how experienced she was.

She folded her arms in front of her chest, determined to keep him wondering, before she realized that her gesture had probably told all.

Ethan said, "Sometimes, not always—but with the right partner—vampires mix the two acts: sex and the drinking of blood. Either of itself is . . . very pleasurable, but the combination . . ."

Parked on the side of a dark road, Kerry didn't like the direction this was taking, even though Ethan was showing no inclination to demonstrate. She said, "I'm sure praying mantises and black widow spiders feel the same."

"Difficult to say." Ethan was close to laughing again, this time *at* her, she was sure. "But it *is* pleasurable for both parties." He shrugged. "Or it *can* be. As with humans, there are always those who take their enjoyment from violence."

"You're saying it's pleasurable because you're a vampire," Kerry said. "If another vampire drinks your blood, you don't die. I think that makes a pretty significant difference."

For some reason that startled him. Then he said, "Kerry, a vampire doesn't kill every time he feeds."

She had no idea whether to believe that.

"A vampire needs to take . . . a little bit more than your

Red Cross does during a blood donation, not much more than a pint. It leaves the human slightly lightheaded, a bit weak. But exhilarated. Even without the sex."

Kerry was skeptical.

"How many vampires do you think there are?" he asked.

That seemed a trap. "I have no idea."

"Good answer." Again the light laugh, which might or might not have been sincere. "But consider: one vampire, one unexplained death per night, how long would it take for people to get suspicious?"

He had a point. She said, "Are you trying to tell me you've never killed anyone?"

"Would you believe that?" he asked, his eyes wide with innocence.

She was tempted, but . . . "No," she said.

"Good." He laughed. "I'm glad you're not that gullible."

"So why do you kill if it isn't necessary?"

"Ah, but it is necessary periodically. Without taking blood, the vampire becomes unable to think of anything besides his all-consuming need, which just grows and grows until eventually he loses what you humans would so arrogantly term 'his humanity.' He becomes like a beast, tearing unthinkingly into the first available victim, and doesn't even recognize until too late if that victim should be his own parent or child or lover. He'll feel devastated, afterward, with their blood coursing through his veins. However, even with a steady diet of blood, too long between kills and the vampire becomes mentally and physically sluggish. He gets weaker and weaker, unable to move, unable to rise out of bed, until finally he's unable even to take the few breaths a vampire needs to survive. It's more than the nourishment; it's the draining of the life force. Feeling the echo of another person's thoughts and memories, which is just as life-sustaining to us as the blood itself. And besides . . ."

She pressed, because he was in a much more open mood than usual. "Besides . . . ?"

"You won't like it." He put the car into drive and pulled back onto the road. "Killing is very pleasurable."

Consider yourself fairly warned, Kerry thought. "So what does all this have to do with Regina?"

"Nothing," Ethan said. "You're the one who brought up vampires' feeding habits."

"You're making me crazy, do you know that?" Kerry said. She could never get the upper hand with him, not even for a minute. She forced the frustration out of her voice, determined not to give him the satisfaction. "So you're saying that another vampire could have killed her, a blood-starved vampire—or just a slightly perverted one—who drained her, then cut off her head to make it look like vampire hunters?"

"No."

"A vampire wouldn't do that?" Kerry asked, between sarcasm and bitterness.

Ethan said, "It was the sun that killed her before the decapitation."

"How can you tell?"

"By how little blood was on the sheets, and the way they were all mussed, as though she struggled. A vampire's sleep is . . . very deep. No restless tossing and turning as in humans' sleep. Sunlight is all that could have wakened her prematurely."

"Not even . . ." It was hard to say out loud. "Not even getting her head cut off?" Kerry asked incredulously.

"There have been such cases," Ethan told her, "and there were no signs of struggle."

He should know. Unless, of course, he was lying. For all she knew, vampires weren't nearly as sensitive to sunlight as he indicated. For all she knew, he could have donned sunglasses and opened the shutters himself. She tried to work it out, with him killing Regina and trying to use her as an alibi when the other vampires came looking, but that seemed needlessly complicated even by vampire standards.

She said, "I assumed you spent the night with her. You know."

He gave her another of those incredulous I-can't-believe-I-heard-you-say-that looks. "Regina and me?"

"I assumed," she repeated, feeling like an idiot.

"No."

Fine, she thought. *But don't pull that Who?-Regina-and-me? routine on me, when you get all twitchy every time her name comes up.* She said, "So these vampire hunters want me because . . . ?"

"Clearly, because you helped me escape and they assume you're one of us."

"Clearly," Kerry repeated. "And what are they likely to have done with my family?"

"That's something else to figure out along the way." Ethan shook his head. "I've been trying to fit Leviticus seventeen-ten into it, and I'm not coming up with anything."

"What?" Kerry asked.

"The message on your wall." Another of those looks. "Beneath the part where they said they had your family."

Kerry remembered there had been letters and numbers she hadn't been able to figure out.

"It's the Biblical injunction against the taking of blood," Ethan explained. "I certainly had it quoted to me enough when they captured me. 'If anyone partakes of any blood, I

102

will set myself against that one and will cut him off from among my people.'"

"The laundry owner," Kerry said. "He's always been real religious. . . ." She saw the look Ethan was giving her and petered off. "You and Regina killed him that night, didn't you? And his wife, and Roth, and Sidowski."

"Sister," Ethan corrected. "You left out Ken Kelada, the one I killed while they were in the process of capturing me. But apparently there was at least one more."

Ken. She remembered the laundry owner on the phone, telling Marcia, "Ken's dead," and Sidowski's accusation: "He broke his neck, just like that." Ethan had denied it, back when it never occurred to her to doubt him. She had thought she was getting used to the idea of violence, but five people dead so far, not counting Regina—

Ethan was watching her. "I told you you wouldn't like it," he said.

CHAPTER TEN

THEY TURNED OFF onto a road that was gravel for a
while, then simply dirt.

"Welcome to Bergen Swamp," Ethan said.

"Looks like woods to me," Kerry said.

Ethan grinned at her. "Ah, but that's until you step into it."

Eventually, when the road was more rutted grass than
dirt, he pulled over to the side.

"What if there are hunters?" Kerry asked. They'd passed
two other cars parked closer to the main road.

"I'll be aware of them long before they see us," Ethan
assured her.

"*Us?*" That was an unpleasant surprise, and she didn't get

out of the car as he opened the back door and flung Regina's remains over his shoulder. Surely he wasn't worried that she'd try to escape when they were miles from anywhere.

"What if there are hunters?" He threw back her own question at her. "Do you want to be alone in the car, trying to explain what you're doing here?"

"I could explain I'm waiting for my . . ." Kerry choked on *boyfriend* and substituted, "someone."

"It might work." Ethan smiled at her. "With certain hunters."

Kerry didn't like the line of thinking that started.

"I'd advise you to stay very close," Ethan said. "Step where I step. Feel free to hold on to the back of my belt. There *are* patches of quicksand."

She scrambled to get untangled from the seatbelt before he got too far ahead. "Wait!" she yelped. One step out of the car and already she was so deep into something that she nearly walked out of her shoe.

Ethan turned around with a glare for all her noise. "Don't—"

"Make a nuisance of myself," she whispered. "I know. I'm sorry. Please don't walk so fast. I can't see as well as you can."

He gave her a chance to get back into her shoe, and when she was ready, she took hold of the hem of his jacket. She did her best to walk as quietly as he did, but even stepping into his footprints she made more noise than he did.

"Are you sure you know where you're going?" she asked.

"Trust me," he said. She was beginning to hate it when he said that. "I've lived in the area all my life. I know every inch of it."

A lot of inches, she thought.

They walked, it seemed, forever. Things scurried just out

of sight—at least out of her sight. The underbrush near them crackled ceaselessly. *Probably best not to ask,* she thought, picturing snakes—which were admittedly unlikely in the middle of the night, with winter setting in—and rabid raccoons. And other vampires. Would Ethan protect her from other vampires? *Could* he?

Finally, in a spot that looked just like every other, Ethan stopped. He set Regina's body on the ground, then stooped down. *Not praying,* Kerry thought—*do vampires pray?*—but studying the land, and the sky, and the land again.

"Is this a good place?" she asked.

"I don't know," Ethan snapped, testy again. He rested his face in his hand. "I've never done this kind of thing before." He pushed the hair away from his forehead, and she saw that his hand was shaking. He sighed. "I have no idea what I'm doing."

Which was both a relief and a concern.

"Never had to dispose of a dead vampire's body before?" she asked.

"Never had a vampire I knew die," he corrected.

Vampire life—with its secret computer messages, and its blue cars, and its absolute dread of the discovery that could doom all—had sounded, despite the potential for immortality, like a fragile, precarious existence. She was surprised he'd never experienced the death of one of his compatriots before.

"Ethan . . ."

He sighed, burying his face in his hands.

"Ethan, how long have you been a vampire?"

He shook his head. "Almost a year," he whispered.

It was not what she expected. It was not at all what she expected. But it explained a lot.

She crouched down beside him and put her hand on his

106

shoulder. Through the leather jacket she could feel his hard muscles but not the coldness of his skin. "How did it happen?"

"I don't want to talk about it." He stood abruptly and took a few steps, but there was no room in which to pace.

With his arms folded and his shoulders hunched, he looked as young and vulnerable as he had that first night.

Finally he said, "My brother and I were driving from the college to the city, to see the New Year's Eve fireworks downtown over the Genesee River. It was my first year away from home. I was a freshman. Peter, a senior." He paused, as though unsure whether to continue.

Whatever was coming next caused him to speak with his teeth on edge. "Out in the middle of nowhere we passed by this car stopped by the side of the road, the hood up, no flares or anything. It was a couple of kids: the girl looked about your age, the boy maybe seventeen, eighteen." Ethan momentarily closed his eyes. "Peter felt sorry for them. He stopped, circled around, pulled up alongside. The girl came to my window. Her eye makeup was all"—he gestured vaguely—"running. She looked like she'd been crying and she said they'd been stuck out there for hours and nobody would stop. So we said we'd take a look, and we got out of our car."

Ethan turned his back to her to compose himself. When he turned back, his voice quavered. "The boy had a gun. He shot Peter three times, and me twice." He shuddered, tightening his arms across his stomach, so Kerry was sure, though he didn't say it, that that was where he'd been shot. "They went through our pockets, took our wallets, and when Peter tried to get up, they shot him one more time, in the head, and drove off in our car. I managed to crawl to Peter's side . . . but he was dead already. I was sure I was going to die, too. And then a car pulled up. I thought it was them again . . ." Once more his voice quavered. "But it was this beautiful lady. Regina. She came and sat down there on the side of the road. She put my head in her lap and stroked my hair, and she told me I was dying, which I knew already. And she told me that, if I wanted, she could stop the pain. And she said, if I wanted, she could help me live." He covered his face and finished the story speaking into his hands. "I was so frightened, I said I wanted to live."

"How awful," Kerry said, hardly able to speak out loud. "Oh, Ethan . . ." She shook her head, knowing that she could never get the words right to let him know how sorry she was. She thought again of everything he'd said and done since they first met, and she realigned it all to fit with this beginning.

And yet . . .

And yet . . .

"But . . . ," she said, "you've been a vampire at least long enough to change your identity once."

He looked at her over his clasped hands.

"You identified yourself as Michael for the other vampires."

"Ah," he said equably, "there is that."

She was no longer hesitant. "And when we were just getting out of the car, you said you'd lived in the area all your life, not that you came here for college."

He shook his head, not looking at all contrite. "You do have me there," he admitted, walking back to Regina's body.

"*Damn* you!" Kerry said.

He just smiled.

She was almost willing to try kicking him for making her feel so wretched.

He waved her back. "I'm going to take her out of the wrappings," he warned.

"I hate you," she said.

"That'll probably work out for the best."

It may well have been the most honest thing he'd said to her so far.

Once more, as he stooped down before the body, she wondered if vampires prayed, or if it would be appropriate to pray for a vampire. But Ethan just tumbled the body out of the wrappings like someone unrolling an area rug to air it out, and Kerry grimaced, unable to look away before making out what she already knew, that there were two separate pieces. Immediately the body and head began to sink in the quicksand.

"There's a creek a few minutes' walk this way." He pointed. "We'll throw the pillow and the nightgown in there." It was the first she realized he must have undressed the corpse back at the house. "We'll drop off the rest of the bedding a little bit here and a little bit there."

"You're so sentimental," she said. "You really need to get ahold of yourself."

He caught her by the ponytail and yanked her back, spinning her to face him. "You don't know anything," he said.

She remembered what it had felt like, in the computer room at Regina's house, when she had first realized he planned to kill her. She'd been foolish to think of him as anything else. *If he lets you live,* she told herself, *focus on what you saw then. Think of him, always, that way.* And not as the sometimes charming, sometimes infuriating companion who chatted to help pass the time; or the open and reasonable vampire who spoke frankly but with some embarrassment about his bloodlust, as though it were a controllable disease; or even the avenging angel who was her family's only hope of survival; and certainly not—especially not—what he'd fooled her with twice already, the poor little waif who only needed to be held and comforted. Whether those were pure fabrications or whether they were, in fact, facets of his personality, the only important one was the one she'd faced in the computer room, the one she faced now.

She could see the glint of his teeth in the moonlight; she all but felt his gaze on her throat. She'd overstepped whatever bounds he'd set for her, and there was no use even trying to struggle.

He bent over her arched neck.

If she had a choice, if it was a matter of letting go or holding on, she was determined to die rather than become a vampire . . .

She felt his lips on her throat.

. . . but where would that leave Dad and Ian?

He kissed her, gently.

"If you don't like vampire games," he said softly, "don't play."

A moment later he released her, so suddenly she almost fell. He tossed her the pillow, the bloodiest of the items, and gathered up the rest, indicating, again, the direction of the creek.

CHAPTER ELEVEN

AT THE CREEK Ethan ripped open Regina's pillow, shaking out a cloud of down before tossing the empty pillowcase into the water.

He dropped the nightgown farther along, then left the creekbed, veering off through the underbrush. They weren't backtrailing, and Kerry could only hope Ethan knew where he was going. She had no sense of where they were in relation to the car.

And Ethan wasn't talking to her. He hadn't said a word—besides "Give me the pillow"—since they'd left Regina's body at the clearing. He was walking faster than she could comfortably keep up with, but she didn't want to hold on to his jacket the way she'd done earlier. And she certainly wasn't going to beg him to slow down when he could easily see for himself she was having trouble. She tramped along behind him, snapping twigs, skidding down embankments with a flurry of dead leaves, uprooting plants when they climbed a steep incline, and puffing open-mouthed with the exertion. She didn't dare let the distance between them grow to more than a few feet or she'd likely misjudge where he'd stepped and land in ground that was boggy rather than just wet. The only way she could keep up was noisily, and if he didn't like it, he could say so.

He didn't say a thing.

She had a chance to catch her breath when Ethan stopped to set one of the sheets on the soggy kind of ground she'd been avoiding. He picked up a rock, big enough that a normal man probably would have had a hard time budging it, and hurled it so that it landed on the sheet. Both began to sink immediately.

Then they were back to walking.

Just when Kerry had begun to give up hope that they'd ever find their way out of the woods, they finally reached the road, the stolen Shadow just a few feet from where they'd emerged.

"What about . . . ?" She gestured vaguely to the other sheet, the comforter, and the quilt he was still carrying.

He threw them into the backseat, which she took as his subtle way of telling her not to worry, that they'd dispose of them later. And, indeed, as they passed through Spencerport—once more heading toward Rochester—he flung the denim jacket out the window without even slowing down.

He still wasn't talking when they returned the Shadow and exchanged it for his original Skylark.

"It'd be interesting," she told him, "to be here when the customer and the mechanics start arguing about the mileage and the half-empty gas tank and all the mud."

Still no answer, despite two attempts at conversation on her part. *Sulking*, she figured. *Be like that*. She crossed her arms over her chest and stared out the window.

She expected that they'd turn around and head back toward Brockport, toward finally doing something about finding Ian and Dad, but he continued on to Rochester. They stopped at an observation point that looked out over the Erie Canal, where he weighted down the second sheet with a rock and threw it into the water. He picked up a few extra rocks, which he tied up in the comforter, but they didn't get rid of that until they were passing over the bridge that spanned Irondequoit Bay.

Kerry checked her wristwatch. It was past 5:00. The last several weeks, her alarm for school, set at 6:30, had gone off while it was still dark outside. She estimated sunrise was about 7:00. Enough time to ditch the quilt and make it back to Brockport, if that was his intent. Not that they could go back to the house he had identified as his uncle's. Whoever had killed Regina had to know about it and could come during the day while he was helpless. She stole a quick glance at Ethan. She seriously doubted he planned to ask her to guard his sleep.

The thought of sleep made her eyes droop. It had been so long since her few hours' worth of sleep Thursday night. After all the running around and emotional strain of tonight, she was surprised, now that she thought about it, that she'd made it this long.

She stifled a yawn, and Ethan glanced at her. Which was more than he'd done the last couple hours.

"Where are we going to spend the day?" she asked in the midst of a second, bigger yawn.

He seemed to be considering not answering, but he finally said, "Rochester subway system."

"Rochester doesn't have a subway," she said.

"It did until the fifties," Ethan told her.

She thought this was good news, that he hadn't gotten confused with Buffalo—since at this point there probably wasn't enough time to get there before dawn. But she couldn't be sure. She didn't even know what to hope for anymore, everything had gotten so muddled.

She asked, "So what happens to an old subway system? Doesn't it get knocked down and filled in?"

"Most of it did," Ethan agreed.

"So this will be underground?"

"Yes."

"And really dark?"

"That's the point."

"I mean really, really dark?"

He looked at her but didn't answer.

Rats, she was thinking. *And assorted creepy-crawling things.* Creepy-crawling all over her while she couldn't even see them. And the kind of people who lived in sewers and on park benches—not just eccentric people like Phyllis, the little old lady who came into the store with cans and bottles she collected for the refunds and who always wore her clothes backward so the CIA would get confused when they tried to follow her—but drug users and escaped convicts and perverts. She remembered, for the first time in hours, the handcuffs, which would guarantee she'd be absolutely unable to defend herself.

Stop it, she told herself. Ethan would hardly choose to

sleep where there were humans about, not while he'd be unable to protect himself.

Rats and creepy-crawling things. She tried to reassure herself that she could make noise to keep them away.

And hope the noise didn't attract the perverts.

Suddenly she wasn't the least bit sleepy.

Ethan pulled into the parking lot of a twenty-four-hour supermarket. "Now what?" she asked miserably as he led her into the store.

"Flashlight," he told her. And, when she looked up hopefully, he added, "I don't need you getting hysterical."

She didn't argue with him about it.

While he picked up two heavy-duty flashlights, the kind with six-volt lantern batteries, to last throughout the daylight hours, she took the opportunity to use the rest room. She half suspected he might demand to accompany her, but whether he was beginning to trust her or was just reluctant to make a scene, he let her go on her own.

Just when she'd decided that it didn't make any difference what she hoped or thought, that she could never escape no matter how she tried.

But the situation hadn't changed. Dad and Ian were still missing, and Ethan was her best chance of finding them.

She relocated him in the video department, watching, of all things, *101 Dalmations*. But he *had* considered that she might not come back, she thought, determined to read human expression into his eyes, into the fact that he linked arms with her.

"In the movies," she pointed out to him, "a vampire could have turned into a bat or mist and followed me."

"In the movies," Ethan countered, "Lassie never peed on the rug."

Arm in arm they approached the cash registers. "Snack?" he asked her.

After he'd been nice enough to provide for light and a bathroom stop, she was sure he was about to do something thoroughly reprehensible. She had the awful feeling he was talking about the cashier. In the bright lights of the store, she saw that he'd lost most of the color he'd had earlier in the evening. Had he eaten—*fed* was the word he'd used— before she ran into him early in the evening? Probably not. The realization hit her that the color she'd seen in his cheeks had probably been from drinking the blood of the laundry vampire hunters last night.

When she didn't answer, Ethan tossed a box of sugar doughnuts on the conveyor belt. "All we've got back in the car is Coke and chips," he reminded her.

But then, as they walked back outside, lest she begin to think too kindly of him, he took her arm and whispered into her ear, as though they were conspirators together, "There were too many people."

Good, she wanted to say. But was it good for her if he got too hungry?

Back on the road, she asked, "Why *did* you buy Coke and chips? Can you eat *some* foods?"

"I entertain," Ethan said. He looked over at her and gave a wicked grin. "Occasionally."

"I see. Sort of like the old witch in 'Hansel and Gretel.' "

"Sort of," Ethan agreed. "It works out especially well with college students. I give them all the beer they can drink. They pass out." He gave her a quick glance, to make sure she understood. "Etcetera."

She didn't like where she had led this, and switched directions. "So where's this subway station?"

"It's not a station."

"Whatever." She leaned her head against the window. The window was cold, but it was warm in the car, and dark, and she had already survived a lot longer than she had originally thought possible, and he hadn't killed anybody in her presence yet, and she only planned to close her eyes for a second . . .

. . . but the next thing she knew there was a bright light, and she was lying down on the ground.

Ethan had hold of her wrist.

She was instantly awake enough to know that he was going to sink his teeth into her arm but not awake enough to fight. Then she felt the cold circlet of metal and heard a click.

She tried to sit but was brought up short because she was handcuffed to a solid-feeling section of track. "You did that," she accused him.

"I did what?"

"You made me fall asleep."

"You were predisposed to anyway," he told her.

They were in a tunnel. There was a lot of rubble but no garbage—probably meaning no people. It was no doubt all for the best that while the glow of the flashlight he'd set by her was bright in their immediate area, she couldn't see very far. The tunnel looked ready to be brought down by a good sneeze.

He set the second flashlight, unlit, right by her hand, in case the first's battery wore down. Her backpack and the bags from the two grocery stores were also within easy reach.

"You didn't want me seeing how to get in here," she said as he sat down cross-legged near her but not near enough for her to be able to reach.

He just smiled.

"Did you carry me?" It was a disconcerting thought, that he'd had her completely helpless. Not that she wasn't completely helpless in any case. . . .

Had he bitten her while she'd been asleep? Would she know? She didn't think she felt weak.

She managed to refrain from touching her neck to check, but he seemed to guess what she was thinking anyway. His smile flickered at the edge of genuine amusement.

"You didn't need me at all, did you?" she asked.

"What do you mean?"

"In the laundry. When I thought I was rescuing you. You could have just . . . used your hypnotic vampire powers—"

"Too much adrenaline."

"I beg your pardon?"

He was having a hard time not laughing at her. "I could have put the thought in their heads that they wanted to sleep, but they were too keyed up and would have resisted."

She sighed. "Were you ever in any real danger from them?"

"Certainly," he answered cheerfully enough.

"But you probably could have escaped without me?"

Ethan made a point of pausing to consider; a mere politeness, she was sure. "I wasn't *incredibly* worried yet," he admitted. "But you had no way of knowing that. And it was very kind of you to want to help."

"You're being too friendly," she told him. "You're making me nervous."

"Good night, Kerry," he said with a laugh, lying down on the ground.

She started to lie down also, but she jumped when she realized Regina's wadded-up quilt was under her head. Even though she couldn't see any blood, she shoved it away in disgust.

Ethan was watching. "You might get cold," he said.

"Not that cold," she answered, though she could already feel the chill seeping into her.

"You're being silly." He closed his eyes and lay still for a moment, but then he took off his jacket and tossed it at her.

"What about you?" she asked, hardly able to keep her teeth from chattering.

He opened his eyes yet again. "Vampires only feel the most extreme temperatures," he told her. "I was wearing the jacket so as not to be conspicuous."

Kerry lay back down, wondering if her sleepiness was his effect or just the last thirty hours catching up. "What about tomorrow?" she asked. She ignored the fact that she was beginning to think like a vampire, marking time by nights rather than days. "What's the plan?"

When he didn't answer, she looked and saw that his eyes were closed. She checked her watch: 7:05. She knew that his heart did beat, although very slowly, during his waking hours. Did it slow down even further, or even stop entirely, by day? She fell asleep before she could figure it out.

CHAPTER TWELVE

KERRY WOKE UP at about 10:00 A.M., her back sore, her right arm—the shackled one—stiff, her toes numb, and the rest of her body aching with cold. The light was still on. No creepy-crawlies in sight, and Ethan hadn't twitched.

Finally she pulled the quilt to her. Without looking closely, she spread it out just enough so she could lie on top. It would protect her somewhat from the cold, hard ground. Any blood, she tried to assure herself, would have been on the sheets and comforter. Still, she was sure she'd never fall asleep again.

The second time she slept, she dreamed about Regina making Ethan into a vampire. She was aware enough to know that she was dreaming and that, anyway, he had already admitted this wasn't the way it had happened.

But she dreamed it the way he had described it.

He was lying by the side of the road, his head on Regina's lap. His expression was frightened and brave and defiant all at once, the same as it had been at the laundry, the darkness of his hair accentuating the paleness of his skin. Regina, looking beautiful but cold and cruel, leaned over him. She tipped his chin up, arching his neck, and set her lips against his throat. She caressed his face and hair gently, but Kerry could see this was only so he wouldn't struggle as she drank his blood. Because it was a dream, Kerry could feel what Ethan felt, which was fear—how could it not be?—and shame, but also pleasure, which was the reason for the shame. Kerry tried to wake herself up but couldn't. His breathing came faster and faster, until, with a shudder of pain, it stopped entirely. Then he opened his eyes.

With that, finally, Kerry woke. It was only early afternoon, but she didn't dare sleep again.

The trouble was, awake, she kept thinking about her family: Was Dad okay? He wouldn't try anything brave and stupid, would he? And how about Ian? Did kidnappers routinely let little kids bring their stuffed koala bears with them? And where was Mom when they needed her?

Best to fill her mind with other thoughts, Kerry decided. Any other thoughts.

The flashlight seemed to be getting dimmer, so she turned on the backup flashlight, turning off the first to conserve the battery in case they got desperate. From her backpack she took out the book she was supposed to have read for literature class. With Regina's quilt wrapped around her, munching on boxed sugar doughnuts and potato chips and sipping Coke, which was as cold as if it had been refrigerated, she finished the story. She hadn't seen a major plot twist coming, and she automatically deducted fifteen points from her potential test score on the basis of an essay answer that made no sense in light of the way the story *had* ended.

Eventually she got bored enough that she not only did her math homework, she started the next unit's assignment as well. *Like I have much chance of ever making it back to school,* she thought.

Ethan woke with a sigh at 4:35.

Kerry would have been willing to bet that if she looked it up in an almanac that would have been the exact moment the sun disappeared beneath the rim of the world. She was about to say "Good morning," but that was ridiculous under the circumstances, and "Good evening" sounded too much like a cartoon version of a Transylvanian count. "Hi," she said.

Ethan sat up, exhibiting none of the slow, gingerly movements *she* had needed before she could move without stiffness. He did give a little stretch, putting his arms around his knees. *See what a couple hundred years' practice sleeping in graveyards will do for your physique,* she told herself.

"Still here," he commented. Hard to tell whether he was surprised.

She held up her arm to show it was still securely shackled to the track.

"I truly hope that wasn't a hardship," he said.

She had found she was most disinclined to believe him when he used words like *honestly* and *truly,* though in this instance she couldn't see what he had to gain by lying. "I was okay," she told him. Even in this light she could tell he was

122

paler than last night, and she didn't want to say anything that might get him annoyed enough to see her as a meal. Not that she estimated he'd need much of an excuse. "What's the next step?" she asked.

He indicated her backpack. "Do you have a change of clothes in there?"

"My school clothes," she answered. "What I wore yesterday." She saw that the cuffs of her supermarket-uniform pants were muddy from their trek through the Bergen Swamp. How had Ethan managed to stay clean? When she sniffed at her blouse, she found that it stank of gasoline. Day-old clothes couldn't be worse than that.

He got the key from his pocket and came to unlock the handcuffs.

"Your hair is longer than yesterday," she said.

"Yeah." He sounded tired, or disgusted. "Our bodies have a tendency to revert to the state they were in when we first became vampires. My hair was longer then. I have to cut it every day, or in two days it's down to my shoulders."

That could be recently, Kerry thought. People wore their hair all sorts of lengths nowadays. On the other hand, she knew the 1960s were famous for boys wearing long hair. She'd seen movies set in the 1950s and was fairly certain short hair was in back then. The only other times she was aware of men wearing long hair were during the Civil War and in colonial times. She really hoped Ethan was from no further back than the '60s.

She rummaged in her backpack and found a spare ponytail elastic for him.

"Thanks." This time he *did* sound surprised. His hair was just long enough that he was able to pull it back into a tight tail.

Kerry thought it made him look like a drug pusher. "You cut it yourself?" she asked.

"Barbers notice things like people coming in every day." Perhaps in repayment for the elastic, Ethan started massaging her wrist to get all the feeling back into it. The corpse coldness of his touch did more to stiffen her muscles than his attempt at being helpful relaxed them. "I was lucky to be well shaved at the time," he added, uncommonly talkative. "When vampires who have beards want to get rid of them, they have to shave two or three times a night."

"That's how your bodies heal," Kerry said, catching on, "by going back to the way they were."

"Which makes it impossible to maintain either a tattoo or a permanent." Ethan let go of her hand. "Not that I've had personal experience with either."

"So when you said that Regina made you a vampire to save your life, even if that *had* been true, it couldn't have been true." She paused, considering whether this had come out making any sense at all. Suddenly she wished she hadn't said it at all. It was too vivid a reminder of her dream.

Ethan seemed to grasp what she'd meant. "It couldn't have happened that way, no. Vampire blood can heal vampires, and our saliva has healing properties, though hardly enough to cure the dying. It's just enough so that if a vampire is careful where and how he bites, somebody might not even know he's been bitten."

Kerry touched her neck, wondering again if he'd taken some of her blood last night when he'd carried her in here.

Ethan grinned at her. "Present company excluded, of course."

Only the paleness of his skin convinced her he was telling

the truth. "Do you plan to?" Stupid question. Of course he'd deny it.

"Take your blood? No." He sat back on his heels and looked at her appraisingly. "Why? Are you intrigued? Do you want to know what it feels like?"

"No," she told him in a voice that she hoped sounded more firm than panicked. She tried to shove the sensations from the dream behind her. "I just want to know what to expect. I figured you probably didn't have time. Yesterday. To"—it was hard to say and he wasn't jumping in to help her, though he must know what she meant—"feed. Before we met."

"I didn't," he said.

When he didn't say anything else, she said, "I didn't think you did."

He flashed another smile at her. "As with living as a human, there's more to being a vampire than feeding," he said. "Surely you can survive a day without food? You probably wouldn't like it, but you could do it."

"Without turning into a beast?" she asked.

"Ah," he said in an adult-to-a-child So-that's-what's-been-worrying-you? tone. "That's after much longer than a day," he assured her. "Besides, if I fed on you, I don't think you'd ever forgive me."

Kerry found it hard to believe he would really be concerned about that.

"And if I did something for which you didn't forgive me," he finished, "I could never trust you again." He stood, one of those disconcertingly fast movements that was hard to follow. "Hurry up and get changed," he said. "There's no reason for both of us to go hungry."

———

AFTER A CONSIDERABLE hike over rubble, they eventually came out at a spot near where the Genesee ran into Lake Ontario. Kerry was amazed to think of Ethan hauling her over all that the previous night, and how she'd slept through it. They left behind Regina's quilt—"In case I ever decide to bring another date here," Ethan told her—but carried out Kerry's backpack and what was left of the groceries.

He took her to a Greek-style family restaurant because, he said, the Greeks generally served breakfast all the time, day and night.

"Why is that?" she asked. "Are there a lot of Greek vampires?"

He just smiled in that way that might mean she'd hit on something he wanted to hide, or that might mean she'd just said something really dumb.

In the restaurant she came back from using the rest room to find Ethan sitting at their table reading a newspaper. "Anything interesting?" she asked when he didn't put it away.

"*Mmm-hmm,*" he said in the same distracted way her father did at the breakfast table. Thinking of her father made her eager to be doing something, and she found herself getting furious at Ethan's slow pace.

"Reading the personals for secret messages from your friends?"

He gave her a dirty look.

She wanted to shake him and scream, *Do something!* but suspected that if she annoyed him too much, he would start moving even more slowly. Determined not to ask any more questions, figuring he wouldn't answer them anyway, she concentrated on her cheese omelet. When she finally looked up, she saw Ethan drinking from the glass of orange juice that was all he'd ordered. "Are you really drinking that?" she asked.

"No, it's all done with mirrors," he answered, still not looking up.

"I didn't think you could."

He did look at her then, peeved. His glance darted about the practically deserted restaurant. "Are you talking about that special diet my doctor has me on?" he asked tightly.

She nodded, delighted to be an irritation to him.

"I *can* have liquids," he told her.

She smiled brightly, but a second later he turned his attention back to the paper.

"Didn't your mother ever teach you it's rude to read at the table?" she asked. It got her wondering if his mother had known he was a vampire. How would her own mother react if she knew what Kerry had done in the last twenty-four hours? If Kerry had been a disappointment before—and she had to have been, or Mom wouldn't have left—the opposite coast wouldn't be far enough should she find out about this.

Ethan brought Kerry back to the East Coast when he answered, "I figured it was all right since I'm reading about you."

"What?" She grabbed for the paper, but he smacked her across the knuckles with it. "What's it say?" she demanded, lowering her voice, suddenly convinced that people *were* listening.

" '. . . disappearance last night of Kerry Nowicki, sixteen, described as having brown hair, hazel eyes, standing about five feet, three inches, and weighing a hundred and twenty pounds.' "

"A hundred and twenty!" Kerry squeaked.

Ethan grinned at her outburst but shushed her. "There's a picture."

He flashed the newspaper in front of her, and she winced.

It was from last year's school yearbook, taken shortly after her mother had left, when—in a fit of depression—she had let her friend Nelle talk her into a home perm.

" '. . . last seen in a pink jacket, white shirt, black pants, and purple apron—' "

Yeah, right, like she'd wear the apron out of the store. She hoped they at least mentioned it was a uniform. "Who reported me missing?"

He motioned her to wait and continued reading. " 'It is not clear whether Kerry ever arrived home after leaving the store parking lot at about eight forty-five in the company of a young man named *Evan*,' "—he gave her a significant look—" 'described as being in his late teens or early twenties, having dark hair, dark eyes, and wearing a vinyl jacket.' *Vinyl*," he scoffed, rolling his blue eyes. "Wonderful witnesses. One of your friends describes you here as 'quiet but friendly' and always having 'a friendly word for everyone.' "

"Who said that?" Kerry asked.

"Craig McDougal, night manager."

"Oh, puke," Kerry said.

"That doesn't sound very friendly."

"What do they say about Ian and my father?"

Again he hushed her.

"What?" she said, seeing him frown. "Ethan!"

"*Shh.*"

She repeated his name in a whisper.

"What bus do you take?"

"What?"

"School bus. Is your driver Cindy Dickerson?"

Kerry shivered. "What happened?"

"An accident that wasn't an accident, involving the bus

and a nineteen eighty-five white Skylark registered to Stephen Nowicki of Fawn Meadow Circle."

"My father?" she asked incredulously, not knowing whether to be relieved or if this was further bad news.

"Your father's car," Ethan corrected. "Is your father in his mid-to-late fifties with a receding hairline and a tendency to wear flannel shirts?"

"No."

"Good." Ethan read, " 'Witnesses say the Skylark side-swiped the bus, driving it off the road near the corner of Brockport Townline Road and Route Thirty-one. The bus skidded along the guardrail for a hundred and fifty feet, with the Skylark remaining in position alongside the bus so that Dickerson couldn't get the vehicle back up on the shoulder. At the point where the guardrail ended, the bus's right front wheel went up over the concrete divider, causing the bus to tip over onto its side and fall into the drainage ditch along the side of the road. Meanwhile the Skylark came to a stop after hitting a fire hydrant.' There's a diagram."

He held the paper up so she could see, but it was hard to focus. "Was anybody"—she couldn't say *killed*—"hurt?"

His blue eyes moved rapidly back and forth as he skimmed the article. "Cuts, bruises, a couple broken arms and cracked ribs. Most of the people were treated at Lakeside, then released. One kid, Kurt Wilmier"—Kerry nodded to show she knew who he meant—"was hit by flying glass and he was taken to Strong Memorial in Rochester. The rest all seem to be in satisfactory condition at Lakeside. They say the bus normally transports forty-five students but most had been dropped off already, so there were only seven still in the bus. The driver of the Skylark took off on foot during the confusion."

"They're saying," Kerry asked, "that it was intentional? The driver of my father's car purposefully . . ."

Ethan was nodding.

Kerry sat back in her seat, stunned.

"The police checked the registration on the car," Ethan said, "and when they went to your house, they found it as we found it. Your neighbor"—he glanced again at the paper—"Mrs. Armendariz thinks your father and brother may have been missing since Friday evening, based on a phone call from you."

Kerry nodded.

"Either they haven't caught on yet—or they just didn't mention—that that's your bus."

"I don't take that bus home on Fridays," Kerry said. "Because of working at the store. But Brockport Townline Road and Thirty-one, that's right before my stop. Do you think this had anything to do with"—Ethan raised his eyebrows at her—"us?"

"If not, I would say that's a fairly incredible coincidence. Our pursuer is beginning to get a face. Or at least a hairline."

"This is not something to take lightly."

"Oh, I'm not taking it lightly," Ethan assured her. "One thing we've learned over the years, the number one rule— after *You can never have too many covers on a window*—is *Don't mess with kids.*"

She remembered the very first night, when he had talked her into not going to the police, arguing that the people from the laundry would never mention her. . . . *"People go crazy when other people hurt kids,"* he'd said. It was to lessen their chances of being found out, but still, she thought, it was one point on the side of the vampires.

"This is awful," she said. "Whoever this is, he risked killing a school bus–load of kids to get at me. What kind of a person would do something like that?"

"Not a very smart one," Ethan said, "if he's after you because he thinks you're a vampire, and he rammed the bus in the afternoon."

Kerry picked up her fork and jabbed it into her omelet several times before she realized what she was doing. She mushed what was left of her food into a soupy mix. "Now what?" she asked.

"We need another car," Ethan said.

Kerry looked at him in shock.

"We'll rent it," he assured her. "It's just at this point I don't know if my name has gotten tangled up in all this."

"You mean because of"—she finally remembered that they were in a public place—"the people from the laundry disappearing?"

He was obviously startled at the suggestion. "No. They didn't disappear. Regina and I made it look like it involved drugs and prostitution."

"*What?*" Kerry asked. "Why?"

"Because that's the kind of thing the police see so often they're the least interested in it. And to keep the families off track."

"The poor families, though." Kerry thought of shocked parents and spouses spending the rest of their lives thinking they'd never really known their loved ones. Like she'd realized she'd never really known her mother.

Ethan shrugged.

"What about Regina's house? Has that been tied in to this?"

"A different article entirely." Ethan turned to the local section. Kerry could read the headline upside down:

SINGLE-FAMILY HOME COMPLETELY DESTROYED BY BLAZE, and underneath that, in smaller print: Fire of Suspicious Origin. Ethan read aloud: " '. . . arson suspected . . . no one hurt in the blaze. . . . The owner wasn't home at the time of the fire, and the police are seeking her for questioning.' "

"So," Kerry said, "nothing specific has you worried, but you're just going to"—she suddenly realized, halfway through the sentence—"drop Ethan Bryne and pick up a new identity."

He didn't answer.

"It must be tough," she said, "living through eternity always having to look over your shoulder."

There was a flicker of annoyance across his face, but before he had a chance to say anything, his attention suddenly shifted to the front door.

Kerry saw a policeman had just walked in. For a moment she thought about jumping up, asking him for help. But how likely was a policeman to believe in vampires? And besides, who was better suited to rescue her father and Ian from vampire hunters—a policeman or a vampire?

Ethan, she was sure, read all of these conflicting thoughts on her face. He gave her a second to be sure of her choice, then: "So," he said breezily, opening the newspaper to the last page, "which is your favorite comic?"

It took Kerry a moment to catch up. " 'Calvin and Hobbes.' "

"That's the morning paper. How about 'Peanuts'?"

"Fine."

The policeman seemed to know the woman who was the hostess, and the cook, who came out from the kitchen wearing a chef's hat and a white apron.

Ethan spread the paper out on the table, and they both leaned over it to read "Peanuts." "Cute," Ethan said.

"*Mmm-hmm,*" she agreed, though she was too distracted for the words to make any sense. Police, or even mall security guards, always made her feel guilty—even when she hadn't done anything. She hoped she didn't *look* guilty.

The policeman was looking around the restaurant, and she was sure he paused an extra few seconds on her.

"I don't get 'Doonesbury,'" she said.

"I never get 'Doonesbury,'" Ethan said.

The policeman was definitely heading toward them.

"Excuse me."

Ethan looked up; and if she hadn't known better, Kerry would have sworn he was startled to find a policeman standing there wanting to talk to them. Startled, but not worried. Curious—the way a perfectly innocent person would be.

"We're looking for a young girl," the policeman said. He even had a picture.

"My God," Ethan said, "she looks just like you, Steffie."

Kerry reached for the picture. It was a copy of the one in the paper. Hesitantly, as though thinking about it, she said, "Naw. Maybe our eyes are the same."

"Oh, the nose, too," Ethan said. "She definitely has your nose." He took Kerry by the chin and tilted her head so she was in profile for the policeman. "Don't you think?" he asked.

The policeman nodded. "The hair's different, of course, curlier and lighter." That had been a side effect of the perm. "May I ask your names?"

"Tim," Ethan said, then corrected it to "Timothy Davin, and my sister."

"Steffie Davin," Kerry said.

"Do you know this girl?" the policeman asked. "Her name's Kerry Nowicki."

"Do we have any Nowickis in the family?" Ethan asked her.

"What's the name of Aunt Fern's daughter's family—the one in Sodus?"

"Noland, I think," Ethan said.

"Well," the policeman said, "then I take it you haven't seen her?"

"I don't think so," Ethan said.

"I don't think so," Kerry repeated.

"Thanks for your trouble." The policeman went back to the hostess and asked if he could set the picture up by the cash register.

"What do you think she's done?" Kerry asked.

"Run away," Ethan answered with a knowing nod.

The policeman left.

". . . or arson, accessory to murder, grand theft auto, and obstructing justice," Ethan finished.

Kerry pushed her plate away. She was becoming an accomplished liar—just as her mother had been those last several months. "What? No credit card fraud?" she asked.

"Ah," Ethan leaned in close to whisper, "that comes when we rent the car."

CHAPTER THIRTEEN

E THAN USED ANOTHER name to rent the car, charging it to MasterCard. He had several MasterCards. The new car was a blue-gray Monte Carlo, rented from a counter at the airport.

"What about the Skylark?" Kerry asked. They were on a fairly busy road, and Ethan slowed to wave ahead of him somebody who was having trouble getting out of a parking lot. That he was a polite driver was just one more thing that didn't fit in with her increasingly confused picture of vampires. "If you just abandon it, surely the police will try to track you down."

"In a few days," Ethan said. "By then, if all goes well, I'll have had a chance to return and cover my tracks. If not . . ."

He shook his head. "I don't like to just drop out of sight—unexplained disappearances generate too much interest—but on the other hand, there won't be anybody pressing the police for answers on my behalf."

If he gets killed, Kerry realized. He was saying what would happen if they succeeded in tracking down the vampire hunter—or if the vampire hunter found them—and he didn't survive the confrontation.

So she wasn't the only one who was worried. Or afraid?

"And what does 'covering your tracks' mean?" she asked. "Fabricating evidence that Ethan Bryne was killed in a drug-related execution?"

She didn't think he was going to answer, but he said, "Possibly. Although I'd prefer to make it look like Gilbert Marsala killed him, probably as part of a Satanic cult ritual. That would explain the message on your living-room wall. The paper didn't mention it, but I'm sure even the Brockport police had to notice it."

Kerry didn't ask what he had against the Brockport police. Instead she asked, "Who's Gilbert Marsala?"

"He's the one who's after us."

She looked at him in stunned silence before managing to ask, "What makes you say that?"

"I recognized his picture in the paper." Before she had a chance to ask, he added: "The police composite. Of the man who rammed the school bus. Didn't I tell you that?" he asked innocently.

"No, you didn't," she snapped. "In fact, you purposefully led me to think otherwise. You made some comment like 'He's just beginning to get a face.'"

"It's hard to resist a good punchline," Ethan said.

"You described him. You didn't say anything about a picture."

"I was summarizing."

Kerry sighed. "Where *is* the paper?"

"I left it at the restaurant. Trust me," Ethan said. "I'm sure it's him. He was Regina's—" He cut himself off.

"What?" Kerry didn't know what to make of his expression. "He was Regina's *what?*"

Ethan glanced over at her but didn't answer. A moment later, he pulled over to the side of the road. He crossed his arms over the steering wheel and buried his face in them. If it had been anybody else, she would have assumed he felt faint or was about to be sick.

Which was an unsettling thought.

Going on his second night without blood, she calculated. He had indicated he could survive longer than that without adverse effects, but since when had she had reason to believe him? "Ethan?" she whispered, not sure she wanted to attract his attention.

Cars whizzed by them. She could feel the Monte Carlo sway with the air of their passing.

Ethan sat back, his eyes unfocused. But then he blinked. He looked at her as if he was about to say something, then changed his mind, and he pulled the car back into the flow of traffic.

Regina again. The mention of Regina always did strange things to him.

It was amazing to realize—with what she knew of both of them—that his reaction could still unsettle her.

Stop thinking of him as human, she warned herself. Every action, every word, every look he gave her was calculated.

And the fact that she couldn't guess *what* they were calculated to do only proved that she was in over her head. *And what about my family?* she wanted to ask. *I keep playing by your rules, and I've been patient,* AND WHAT ABOUT MY FAMILY?

But she could picture him, in the mood he was in, whirling around and slapping her and telling her to stop whining.

Mile after silent mile they drove. They were once again on the road between Brockport and Rochester. Kerry was beginning to actively and passionately hate that road.

Just outside of the village, Ethan pulled into a minimart parking lot, stopping the car at the phone booth tucked in the corner.

"Who are you calling?" she asked, breaking the silence that had hovered between them like an ominous third person. Like the ghost of Regina.

Instead of answering, he said, "Take off your jacket." She did, and he tossed it into the backseat and gave her his.

"Why?" she asked.

"The police here will be searching for you more actively than the Rochester police were, and the description they have says you were wearing a pink jacket."

"Yeah, but it also says I'm wearing black pants."

"I don't want them noticing you," he said. "I don't want them looking that closely at you."

"Yeah, but—"

"Would you take the damn jacket?"

She took it, though she thought people would be more likely to notice him without any jacket at all—it was about thirty degrees, and all he had on was a white dress shirt and jeans.

He got out of the car and she followed him to the phone. "Who are you calling?" she asked again.

Still he didn't answer, but he called Information, since vandals had cut the chain where a phone book should have been attached. "I'd like the phone number and address of Gilbert Marsala," he said.

Kerry was standing close enough to hear the operator say she could give out the phone number but not the address.

"All right," Ethan said reasonably, "I just wanted to make sure I got Gilbert Marsala *Junior* and not Gilbert Marsala Senior."

The operator said, "We have only one listing, sir, which doesn't specify 'Junior' or 'Senior.' The address is on Canal Street."

Ethan winked at Kerry, and in a very concerned voice said, "The old man lives on Canal Street, too."

"This is at one-forty-seven Canal Street," the operator said. She was beginning to sound a bit impatient, Kerry thought. She was probably supposed to handle calls in a certain number of seconds, and Ethan was dragging this out, ruining her average.

"That's the one," Ethan said. "Thank you very much."

He didn't bother writing down the phone number, which meant either he had a very good memory or he didn't care.

Back in the car, Kerry finally, warily, asked what she'd been wondering since Rochester. "Ethan, just who is this man?"

Ethan looked startled, then flustered and at a loss for words, a first for him. "I'm sorry," he said, another first. "I forgot that I"—*Freaked out at the mention of Regina?* Kerry supplied mentally—"never told you. He's a professor at the college. He teaches English composition, both day classes and CE."

Kerry looked at him blankly.

"Continuing Ed." Her look must not have improved. "At night."

"Oh," she said. Then, "Oh. You mean Regina really *was* a teacher."

She hadn't meant to bring up Regina yet again, but Ethan was grinning at her. "Yes. And I really was a student. Neither of us full-time, of course. Anyway, Marsala was the adjunct coordinator for CE and Regina had to report to him. She pointed him out to me one night when there was a blizzard warning and all the other teachers were letting out early. He was the only one who insisted on his students staying for the full lecture. Boring little man—should have just let them go."

"You don't like English composition?"

Ethan shrugged.

Kerry took a deep breath and asked the important question. "Do you think he has my family?"

"Yes."

Finally, an unequivocal answer. She pressed on. "At his house or someplace else?"

"Hard to say."

"What are we going to do," Kerry asked, "when we get to his house?"

Ethan gave her another grin.

"You're not going to tell me because I'm not going to like it?" she guessed.

His expression softened to a more honestly amused smile, but he still didn't answer.

"I hate when you do that," she told him. She put her back to him, determined not to answer any of his questions—if he asked her any—and stared out the window till they reached Canal Street.

It was just after 6:30. Lights were on; most people were

probably still preparing for or cleaning up after dinner. Number 147 turned out to be the one house that had no lights. It was a single-story house, much too ordinary looking a place for its owner to have chopped off someone's head and run a school bus off the road.

Ethan slowed almost to a stop, then cruised past.

"What are we doing?"

"Circling the block."

The next time around, he pulled up in front of the house. The lights were still off.

"Nobody's home," Ethan said.

"Was the plan to knock on the door and ask to go in?" Kerry asked.

He looked at her but didn't answer.

"My father and brother could be in there. Prisoners. He wouldn't have left a light on for them. He'd leave them in the dark." She didn't add that Ian was afraid of the dark.

"I'd hear their heartbeats," Ethan said.

"From out here? With the engine running?" If they weren't here, *where were they?*

"Yes," Ethan said.

"Even if they're in the basement? Even if they're in a closet in the basement? You know, maybe one of those cedar-lined closets with big, thick walls, so—"

"Kerry, they're not there. Nobody is." He pulled away from the curb.

"No!" she said.

He grabbed hold of her by the shoulder, perhaps thinking that she was planning on opening the door and jumping out. Which wasn't a bad idea, she thought. "We'll park farther down the street," Ethan said.

It took a few moments for the meaning to sink in: They *were* going in.

"All right?" He looked at her apprehensively. "We'll leave the car where he won't see it when he comes home and get suspicious."

She nodded, still afraid that he just wanted to get her out of there quietly.

He finally let go of her.

Somebody on the next block was having a party. Cars were parked on front lawns of houses on either side of the road for a four- or five-house stretch. Ethan just pulled in, the last in line on the right-hand side.

If he could hear heartbeats from inside houses, he must be able to hear hers now, Kerry knew. He must be able to tell it was going at a frantic rate; he kept giving her anxious looks, perhaps concerned that she would panic and get hysterical or do something desperate and stupid.

They walked back to 147, right up the front walk, to the front door. Ethan pulled his lock-picking tools out of his pocket as calmly and matter-of-factly as an accountant going for pen and calculator, the image reinforced by his clean-cut good looks and white shirt. He had a pair of thin gloves in the pocket with his tools, and he pulled these on before setting to work.

She heard the click of the lock opening. "Don't touch anything," Ethan warned as though she were too dumb to know about leaving fingerprints, and in a moment they were in the dark entryway. The house turned out to be a raised ranch, so that they were faced immediately with a decision between two sets of stairs, one going up to the living area, the other leading to the basement.

Ethan pushed the door shut behind them. Standing there,

waiting for her eyes to adjust themselves to the dark—which they never would, not to the extent that his already had—he said, "They're not here."

"Could they be"—she'd had the thought so long, she was able to say it—"dead?"

"Not here," Ethan repeated.

He'd told her before that he could smell a quantity of spilled blood. How much constituted "a quantity"? On second thought, she didn't want to think about that.

He took her hand, leading her through the house, probably just as much to acquaint himself with the setup as to reassure her.

The basement, the first place they looked, was empty compared to Regina's. There were neatly stacked boxes, whose labels she could read from the glow of the neighbor's driveway floodlight: HALLOWEEN, CHRISTMAS, EASTER, THANKSGIVING. Even, way down at the bottom, one marked ST. PATRICK'S DAY, though "Marsala" certainly didn't sound Irish.

"No Valentine's Day," Kerry observed. "No Mrs. Marsala?"

"I think she ran off to Tahiti or something two or three years ago. Before I came to Brockport."

Kerry was distracted by the realization that the Nowickis and the Marsalas had something in common. She thought of her own mother, somewhere in Florida. Had the police contacted her to tell her that her family was missing? Did she care? "There is a Marsala Junior though?"

"Not . . . ," Ethan started, but then he spotted what she was looking at, a child's Bigwheel, parked on top of a stack of boxes all marked JOE or JOEY: JOE'S BOOKS, JOE'S TROPHIES, JOEY'S SCIENCE FAIR PROJECT, JOEY'S SCHOOL PAPERS, CLOTHES—JOE'S. ". . . that I ever heard of," Ethan finished.

143

He ran his gloved finger across the top box. The light wasn't bright enough for Kerry to be able to see, but the way he rubbed his fingers afterward told her there was dust.

"What's the matter?" she asked because he seemed to be spending a lot of energy thinking about something.

He shook his head and finished the circuit around the basement: laundry area, including what looked to be a sauna room; window screens leaning against the wall; four dusty bicycles, then the furnace, and so back to the stairs, where Ethan nudged her.

"What?" she demanded. "I can't see a thing."

"Do you see the shelves under the stairs?"

"Yeah . . . ?"

"Do you see the spray can of red paint?"

Kerry stepped forward, trying to make it out in the dark, but she knew enough not to get her fingerprints on it. "Lots of people use red paint," she pointed out. But she was convinced.

"We don't even have to plant evidence," Ethan said, obviously pleased with himself and the world. "Shall we check upstairs?"

Upstairs revealed nothing that seemed important to Kerry. There were three bedrooms. The master bedroom had a huge walk-in closet, which was practically empty—just four or five shirts, a couple pairs of pants, a tweed sports jacket, and one pair of dress shoes. Apparently Professor Marsala hadn't adjusted very well to his wife's leaving. The second bedroom seemed to be a library—a lot of books, mostly nonfiction. The third bedroom, whose door had been closed, was empty. A rug and drapes, but absolutely nothing else— not even a light.

The kitchen had what looked to be breakfast dishes in

the sink and a package of chicken breasts on the counter. The package had leaked, and when Kerry poked at it, she discovered it was not only thawed out, it was room temperature.

Looking exasperated with her, Ethan used his glove to rub at the spot she had touched. *Fingerprints,* she remembered.

"He didn't come home last night," she said.

"Doesn't look like," Ethan agreed.

"Is that good news or bad for my family?"

"I don't know."

"Do you think he was injured in the accident?" An awful thought struck her. "What if he has them someplace and he's died and they can't get out, and they're running out of food, maybe they're running out of air—"

"Kerry." Ethan shook his head. "There was nothing in the paper about his being injured."

"Then where is he? And where is he keeping Dad and Ian?"

"I don't know."

The living room had more books. No tapes, records, or CDs, but a piano, with its cover closed and pictures where the sheet music would go. Kerry guessed that whoever used to play the piano no longer did, or no longer lived there.

Ethan picked up one of the framed pictures. Kerry looked at it over his shoulder. A man who might be Professor Marsala stood with his arm around a young man who looked enough like him that Kerry suspected he was Marsala's son—Joe, she supposed. Joe wore a T-shirt that read: BROCKPORT HIGH SCHOOL CROSS COUNTRY TEAM and he was holding aloft a trophy. Both men were smiling. Joe, especially, had an infectious smile.

Ethan put that one down and picked up another that was

lying face down on top of the piano. Joe again, this time wearing huge white rabbit ears, a waistcoat, and a pocket watch. Behind him was a poster that said *Alice!* Kerry remembered going to the student production with her class three years ago. It took her several seconds to realize that the woman holding possessively on to Joe's arm—the one wearing the sweatshirt proclaiming, BECAUSE I'M THE DIRECTOR, THAT'S WHY—was Regina.

Ethan studied the picture silently for several long seconds, then suddenly brought it down sharply against the edge of the piano.

"Sorry," he said, seeing her jump. The momentary flash of rage on his face disappeared, and he tossed the smashed frame to the floor.

"You know him?" Kerry asked. "The young man?"

"Never saw him before," Ethan answered with a straight face.

She felt her own flash of rage. She was furious about all Ethan's evasions and lies. But what were her options? Her dependency on his goodwill, her inability to survive on her own—were driving her into a fury. *And what about Dad and Ian?* she wanted to scream at him. *What about what YOU promised ME?*

Ethan said, "Come. Surely after yesterday Marsala suspects that we, or the police, have guessed who he is. He won't be back. There's nothing for us here."

CHAPTER FOURTEEN

IN THE CAR once more, Ethan sat back in the seat, staring straight ahead, without turning on the engine.

When she could stand it no longer, Kerry asked, "Now what?"

"I don't know," he admitted.

It was a terrifying thought. She expected him to lie and to not tell her things. But at the same time, she assumed he'd know what to do in every situation. *Ethan?* At a loss?

After a long moment, she said, "Somebody's going to start wondering about us just sitting here. Where should we go next?"

He shook his head.

Enough was enough. "Where would he be?" Kerry

demanded from between clenched teeth. "Obviously he wants me to find him. That's why he took my family: to get to me. What good does it do him to hold my family hostage if I can't give myself up to him?"

Ethan rubbed his forehead as if she were giving him a headache. "I don't know."

"Maybe we should go back to my house," she suggested. "Maybe he's left another message there."

Ethan considered. "All right," he said in a since-we-don't-have-anything-better-to-try tone.

They drove to Fawn Meadow Circle, where Kerry found her house surrounded by yellow plastic Crime Scene tape.

"Nobody here," Ethan said, and in the next breath, before she could protest, "We'll circle around to the back. Under the circumstances, your neighbors would be sure to report a strange car parked in the circle."

He parked instead on Frandee Lane, a block away from the Hill family's house, whose yard they cut through to get into her own backyard.

"My key's only good for the front door," Kerry said, but by the time she'd finished saying it, Ethan had jimmied open the sliding-glass door and was ducking under the police tape that blocked this entry, too.

It was a strange sensation, sneaking through her own house. Distracted, she took several moments to register the state of the rooms. They were perfectly normal. Family room, kitchen, dining room—nothing was out of the ordinary in any of them. It was only in the living room that she found what she remembered and expected, the furniture toppled and slashed, the broken lamps on the floor.

"He only ransacked this room," she pointed out in a whisper, as though Ethan could have missed it.

"*Ransacked* implies he was looking for something," Ethan said, whispering, as she had. "I can't think what he could have been looking for. More likely he was just trying to get your attention, prove that he meant business."

She put her hand out to touch the wall spray-painted with the words, VAMPIRE, WE HAVE YOUR FAMILY.

Ethan caught her wrist and shook his head.

Fingerprinting powder, she realized. The walls, the furniture, everything was thick with black dust where the police had checked for fingerprints. She didn't need to touch the wall, anyway. The message was just as she had remembered it: VAMPIRE, WE HAVE YOUR FAMILY. And, beneath that, LEV 17:10. She realized what she had subconsciously been hoping for was that a second message would have been added: *Come to the Newman Chapel at midnight*, or *Meet us by the cemetery gate*, or *We'll be at the laundry where it all started*. "Do you think there's really more than one of them?" she asked. "Or is the 'we' only to throw us off?"

"I thought there were only five of them to begin with," Ethan said, by which she took him to mean he didn't have any idea.

She spotted Ian's bear, Footy, on the floor, half under a couch cushion, and all the courage and resolve ran out of her. She knelt on the floor to pick him up and began to cry, rocking back and forth, unable to stop.

Ethan gave her about fifteen seconds. "Kerry. Kerry, there's nothing here." He took the bear from her and set it back down. "If the police return, we don't want them to know somebody's been in here." He forced her to get up, walked her through the house to the back door. But he gave her another few seconds to stop crying, so that her noise wouldn't attract the neighbors' attention.

Back in his car once again, he handed her a handkerchief, and she asked, "Do you think they could have left a message at your house?"

He hesitated. "No."

"Well, we know they can't have left one at Regina's," she snapped, remembering all the gasoline and seeing again the dark smoke rising in the night sky.

No answer.

"You each had more than one house, didn't you?" she asked. "Different places bought under different names so that if you felt one was unsafe, you could go to another. Damn vampire caginess."

Still no answer.

"And you're afraid to let me in on your secrets."

He didn't like her use of the word *afraid*, she could tell.

"You're *afraid* that if somehow I get away from you, I know too much already, and I'll be a threat."

He didn't deny it. He didn't even deny the implication that her *getting away* was the only way they'd part company.

"Damn it"—she wasn't in the habit of swearing and realized she was doing more in his company than she ever had previously—"Marsala is missing, my family is missing, and all you're interested in is maintaining vampire secrets."

"Do you want out?" he asked very, very softly, so that she could have no doubt exactly what he was asking.

"I want to find my family." Her voice came as a frightened squeak.

"And I want to find Marsala," he said. "Help me get to him, and we'll find your family."

"Where do we look?" she repeated yet again.

"Where would you go," he asked, "if you were a vampire hunter whose plans were going awry, whose companions had been killed, who knew there was a good chance the vampires knew who you were—where would you go at night?"

"You make it sound like he isn't looking for us."

"I don't think he is, not at this point. I think he's hiding."

"Then we'll never find him!" she cried in dismay.

"Depends. Vampires have a lot of experience hiding. This guy hasn't. He'll stay in Brockport rather than go to Rochester, where he'd have more options—"

"Why?"

"*Why* will he stay in Brockport, or *why* would he have more options in Rochester?"

"Both."

Ethan started the car, which she thought meant she'd asked one question too many and he wasn't going to answer any. But he just must have been getting nervous about hanging around her neighborhood too long and attracting the attention of someone who might recognize her.

"He'll want to be with people. He'll figure, rightly, that a vampire wouldn't walk into a crowded room, grab hold of him, and kill him in front of witnesses. A vampire's main defense is the general public's lack of belief in vampires."

"A vampire could shoot a person," she said, speaking in a general sort of way and trying very hard not to think of specific vampires hurting specific people, even if those specific people had hurt her family, "or run him over, or push him out a window, or kill him in some other nonvampire way so that witnesses—"

"And get away and elude the police, also in some non-vampire way. It's possible. But, still, his best chance is going to be in a crowd."

"All right," Kerry conceded.

"The trouble is—for him, of course—that vampires are

used to hunting in the night, and most humans live in the daylight. In a big city like Rochester, he could have his choice of well-populated nightspots."

"But you don't think he's gone to Rochester."

"One," Ethan said, "he knows Brockport better than he knows Rochester. Two, he has friends in Brockport. They may not be good-enough friends to trust with his suspicions that there are vampires, but if we do come after him, he'll be more inclined to trust his life with people who know him than with strangers in a city, who might just turn their backs at the first sign of trouble. Three, if he's to have any chance at all to catch us, he knows you won't leave Brockport, because of your family. Four, I can't have been the only person to recognize him—"

"More reason to lose himself in Rochester," Kerry interrupted.

"He won't have run. Not if he ever expects to come back to Brockport. The police have already questioned him. He's pointed out that he has no motive at all to harm your family or the passengers on the school bus—and, in fact, he doesn't even know any of you; he's a respected member of the community; he wasn't anywhere near the school-bus crash. Right?" he asked.

She nodded.

"But still, he looks remarkably like the man who did it. The police have questioned him, they've told him to stick around, so if he suddenly starts taking off for Rochester every night, they're going to get suspicious."

Kerry sighed. "Does all of this bring us any closer to knowing where he is?"

"Well, we've just eliminated Rochester."

"Wonderful."

"And the Brockport possibilities will reduce drastically as the night wears on: stores in the plazas will shut at nine, most restaurants around midnight, bars at two . . ."

"Some restaurants are open twenty-four hours," Kerry said. "And both supermarkets."

Ethan nodded. "The Student Union stops serving alcohol at two, but the cafeteria is open all night. The dorm lobbies always have somebody around."

"The college clinic," she added. "Where do we start?"

"None of them. It's not even seven-thirty. He isn't going to hang around just one place between sunset and dawn—that's more than twelve hours. That would raise too many questions. At this point, he could be anywhere. We'll start looking as it gets later."

"What about my family?" she asked, then pointed out, "People would surely notice if he was dragging two prisoners around with him. He can't have them with him."

Ethan briefly closed his eyes, as though weary of hearing about her family. "Obviously not," he agreed.

And that was all he said.

He thinks they're dead, she thought. She refused to believe it, as though her hope alone could prevent it from being so. "Well, then," she said calmly and evenly, so as not to rile him, "where will we go until it's time to start looking?"

"My house." He gave her a sidelong glance. "The one you know. I might have been wrong: there might be a message there."

She raised her eyebrows. First an apology for not telling her about Marsala, then an acknowledgment that he might be wrong, both in the same night. She went from pleasantly surprised to alarmed as the thought occurred to her that he might have given in for some reason she couldn't guess, some reason that would mean no good for her.

THEY DROVE AROUND his block twice, to make sure no one was parked or hanging around nearby watching.

"No heartbeats?" Kerry asked.

"No heartbeats," Ethan acknowledged.

Also no messages.

At least, none in the living room, which was where Ethan led her and which, presumably, was the only part of the house he was willing to have Kerry see. It was the same room she'd been peeking into the night she'd first come here, the night this had all started. It was hard to believe that was Thursday and this was only Saturday.

The decor was elegant—rich, but much more subdued than at Regina's. *Old money* was the phrase that came to Kerry's mind. She wondered if the house reflected Ethan's tastes or those of the previous owner. Was there an uncle, vampire or not? Or had Ethan himself owned the house all along, coming and going every generation or so, staying only so long as it wouldn't be apparent that he wasn't aging? That would be a shorter time for him than it would have been for Regina, who could have passed—stretching just a bit—anywhere from late twenties to early forties. Ethan probably wouldn't be safe for more than five years in any one location, which had to be a serious inconvenience. She found herself wondering, not for the first time, whether he had somehow chosen to become a vampire, or had the choice thrust upon him by someone else.

Either way, she thought, *they should have waited.* What was it like to pull up roots every five years, to have to get used to a new place, make new friends?

She realized she was thinking like a human rather than a vampire. His friends were all vampires, for whom he didn't have to pretend. The humans of his acquaintance would be nothing more to him than potential meals.

Thinking of his meals made her uncomfortable, here, alone with him, as he sat on a chair across from her, watching her silently. Was that why he had brought her here?

She stood, and his gaze followed her as she walked nervously around the room, stopping, eventually, at the piano. No dust, but no music on the rack, either. "Do you play?" she asked.

"Yes."

Her mother had taken her to Suzuki piano lessons from the time she was five till, worn out from fighting about practice, Mom had let her drop it at age eight. *How much would it have hurt,* Kerry asked herself, *to practice fifteen minutes a day?* Would Mom have run off to Florida if Kerry had been a better daughter? Kerry positioned her right hand over the keys and played the first thing she had learned and the only thing she remembered: "Twinkle, Twinkle, Little Star," each note played six times to the beat of the phrase "Mississippi hot dog."

"It'll be a long night if I'm in charge of entertainment," she said.

Ethan came and sat on the piano stool. He played a classical piece, something very lively and complicated that sounded vaguely familiar, as though it had possibly been used as part of a movie's soundtrack.

"Beethoven?" she asked, which was the only classical composer who came to mind.

155

Ethan winced. "Mozart."

She couldn't guess if he didn't like Beethoven or if he just thought she should have known the difference.

"Was he from your time?" she asked.

"Mozart's timeless." He began playing something different. "*This* is Beethoven."

"How are vampires made?" she asked.

Playing the piano wasn't enough distraction to let him be caught off guard. "There's absolutely no reason for you to know that."

"Professor Marsala seems to think it's a process that takes place over time, that I can be part vampire and yet still human enough to ride by day on a school bus. Either that, or he thinks *you're* part of our family, and the message was meant for you all along, and not me."

"Professor Marsala is wrong," Ethan said. "Either way. The *process* of becoming a vampire takes all of a few seconds." He switched midmelody to a hyperkinetic version of the already fast "Minute Waltz," then switched again, this time to the Righteous Brothers' slow and haunting "Unchained Melody."

Kerry wondered if the length of time he'd played "The Minute Waltz" was the actual amount of time it took to change from human to vampire, or if he just couldn't keep up the pace.

"Familiar with this?" Ethan asked. "The words were written by a human—as far as I know—but it *sounds* like a vampire song."

She thought he might sing, but he didn't. "Do you choose?" Kerry asked. "To become a vampire? Or is it like an infection?"

"Oh, there's a choice," Ethan said. "There's always a choice. To one extent or another." He rested both arms on the keyboard, creating a discordant jumble of notes that was especially jarring in the middle of the soft melody he'd been playing. "Sometimes people become aware there are vampires in their midst, and they seek to become one. For the power. For the immortality. Believe me, you've seen the worst of it these last two days; it *can* be a seductively appealing life. Sometimes, after one of a pair of lovers becomes a vampire, the other may choose to become one also."

Regina? Kerry wondered. "Sometimes . . . ," she urged him to continue.

Ethan gave a tight smile. "Are you aware that you can't kill yourself by holding your breath? Your body needs the oxygen and unless you're holding something in front of your face that blocks your mouth and nose so that it's suffocation instead of breath holding—unless you're doing that, eventually your body takes over for your mind and takes that breath. Sometimes the choice is like that."

"To die, or to become a vampire," Kerry said. Some choice.

"The vampire who made me," Ethan said, "drank my blood to the point where I was dying. I hadn't known before then that he was a vampire."

"*He?* You mean it wasn't Regina?"

"I thought we discounted that story ages ago." Ethan sounded surprised she'd believed any of it. "I knew, as I lay there with my heart straining to continue pumping what little blood remained, what he was. And I knew, when he bit his own wrist and held it out to me, what he was offering. Not the details, of course. But I knew. And I chose." He held his arms out in an and-here-we-are gesture. "Not everybody makes the same choice, of course. But there's no way a vampire could force enough of his blood down a victim's throat against the victim's will. So there *is* a choice."

He put his fingers back on the keyboard and began playing ragtime.

Which seemed a deliberate effort to change the mood.

Which Kerry thought was a very good idea. "Is *this* from your time?" she asked.

"Joplin? No."

"Good," she said. "Now we're getting somewhere. Was he born before or after you? And if you choose to answer that, could you also tell me when *was* Joplin born?"

Ethan laughed.

"Is there any way to stop being a vampire?"

"Certainly."

Kerry considered, then asked, "Any way that doesn't involve killing the vampire?"

Again the laugh, more genuinely amused this time. "That *does* make it more difficult." But then, after a moment, he added, "Yes. So, you see, there are choices after choices."

"Something finally occurred to me," Kerry said, "during one of our long, silent rides."

He was good enough to be able to watch her without missing a beat of the complicated syncopated rhythm.

"I thought Regina was French because she called you *mon cher*, but that was absolutely all she ever said in French. You, however, swore in French when you were so upset you forgot yourself."

He continued playing, continued watching her, not looking at all upset at the mention of Regina. Did he periodically throw fits and tantrums just to keep her off balance? she wondered.

"So," she said, "I figure you're French, or were originally."

In the middle of the ragtime piece, he played the opening measures of "La Marseillaise," the French national anthem, giving it, too, a ragtime beat before switching back to the original tune.

"But you've been here long enough to lose any trace of an accent."

"Does this speculation eventually lead somewhere?" he asked.

"I was just wondering, which is older, you or America?"

"Ah," Ethan said, "are you referring to Columbus's discovery of America or Leif Eriksson's?"

The question left her breathless, to think that Ethan was somewhere between 350 and 1,000 years old.

"Joke," he said, seeing her face.

But she wasn't sure that it was.

And, in any case, he never did answer her question.

CHAPTER FIFTEEN

I T WAS PAST midnight when Kerry couldn't take the waiting any longer. "You don't have to say it," she said. "I know I'm not going to like it—but what's the plan?"

Ethan paused the tape to which he was listening and lifted the headphones from his ears. "What?"

He was learning, he had said, conversational Japanese, though he wasn't practicing out loud. No doubt he was too arrogant to risk stumbling over pronunciations in front of a witness, even a witness who wouldn't have any idea how far off he was. She figured this was final proof, if she needed more, that he was incredibly old. She knew she'd have to be incredibly old before she'd spend her time teaching herself Japanese.

Kerry suspected that he'd intentionally plunked her down in front of the TV on a night with no good shows so that she'd be bored enough to fall asleep while he pursued his own quiet activities. She'd had enough sleep during the day, she told herself; her eyes were getting droopy simply out of force of habit, because it was past midnight. *I will not give him any opportunities,* she told herself. Even fighting would be better than the risk of sleeping while he was awake.

"The plan," Kerry repeated. "Is there one?"

Ethan glanced at his watch, then put the headphones down and turned off the tape recorder completely. "I was planning," he said, with just the slightest emphasis on the word *planning,* "to throw you to the wolves."

"Could you be more specific?" Kerry asked with what she considered admirable calm.

"You said, when you first agreed to help me, that you could go places I couldn't. This is one of those occasions. If we walk into whatever place Marsala has barricaded himself, he's likely to do something foolish."

"Like?" She had a scene in mind straight out of Saturday-morning cartoons, with the professor sitting on boxes labeled TNT and DYNAMITE, holding the detonator on his lap.

Ethan shrugged. "Something loud and attention getting. He might accuse us of being the ones who caused the accident with the school bus, or admit that he was the one but claim that it was in an attempt to capture us—for whatever reason he might think up to accuse us—and he'll demand that the police be summoned. Or he might start shouting that he has proof that we killed Regina—or at the very least burned down her house. I don't know; he might claim that I picked his pocket or you propositioned him, or he saw us trying to steal money from a cash register. Whatever. Something to cause a scene, to focus attention on us. And to keep the attention on us till sunrise."

"Okay," Kerry said. "I follow so far."

"That's if the two of us walk in together."

"This is the throwing-me-to-the-wolves part, isn't it?" she asked, trying to make light of it.

Ethan gave her a grin that was rather wolfish itself. "If you go in by yourself, he's not going to do any of that, because even if you burn up in front of everyone's eyes he's blown everything to get you. But he hasn't laid a finger on me. I don't think he's going to be satisfied with that."

"And you can't go in alone, instead of me, because . . . ?"

"Well, I could say because I suspect he doesn't really believe you're a vampire, that he's used you to get to me and that he doesn't care one way or the other what becomes of you."

Kerry returned his patently insincere smile. "Or you could say . . . ?"

"Because I personally am not willing to risk it. Take your pick."

"I like the first better," Kerry said.

"So do I," Ethan agreed cheerfully.

"Assuming we—I—find him, then what?"

"You convince him that you escaped from me. You can tell him that I fed on you. I could leave a mark." He reached across the table faster than she had time to react to and brushed the back of his fingers across her neck. She jerked away instinctively, even though she knew he could have stopped her if he wanted. "Or not," he added with his vampire smile. "But: you hate me, I do despicable things, I've forced you to watch me feed on babies, I've raped you, I'm planning

162

on overthrowing the government. I'm sure you can think of some reason."

They stared at each other across the table, him daring her to admit it. Or deny it. The more she thought about it, the less sure she was. "I tell him I hate you . . . ," she prompted.

He smiled at her equivocal answer. "And ask him to help you get me. He will, of course, tell you all manner of lies."

"Unlike you."

"He might say he never kidnapped your family, that the vampires did that."

It had crossed her mind. She hadn't met Ethan till after eight-thirty, which would have given him four unaccounted-for hours between rising and running into her at the store.

He was watching her as though trying to gauge her response. "Or he might say that he talked to your father and convinced him of the danger you ran by associating with me. Your father agreed to help, and he and your brother are perfectly safe and in hiding. Hiding from me, Satan's demon spawn. Or he might say that he took them but then let them go. Out of the goodness of his heart, one presumes. He has a good heart: he never intended to cause the bus accident, but a vampire drove him off the road and the next thing he knew he'd accidentally hit the bus."

"It was in the afternoon," Kerry reminded him.

"Maybe it was a bee, then. In any case, he *will* try very hard to turn you against me, and I'm sure he'll be very convincing."

"I find him," Kerry summarized, "tell him I hate you, listen to his lies but don't let them sway me from my purpose. . . . I *do* have a purpose, don't I?" *I could get killed,* she reminded herself, *despite Ethan's assurances.* But what chance did any of them have if she was too frightened to act?

Ethan said, "Our purpose is to get him out of his public hiding place." Before she could ask *How?* he said, "Tell him that you overpowered me."

"Yeah, like he's going to believe that.

"I tied you up before dawn, but you got loose while I was still asleep in my coffin, and you secured the lid shut so I couldn't get out—"

"Do you sleep in a coffin?" Kerry asked.

"No. —and you've been looking for him ever since. Which, you tell him, was what *I* planned to do tonight. So you've gone to him, first to warn him, second because he's the one person in the world who'll believe you about me, third to have him do your dirty work for you."

"Meaning, to kill you." Obviously. "And where will you be all this time?"

"My house, which is where you'll tell him I am. Except that I won't be in the helpless heap he anticipates."

"Will you kill him?" Even though she knew that Marsala might well have injured or killed her family, that went against everything she had ever believed in.

"My God, Kerry," Ethan said, "that can't be a surprise."

"No," she admitted.

"As it can't be a surprise that, given the chance, he'd kill me. And no matter what he tells you tonight, he'll be planning to kill you, too."

Ethan looked so calm, so matter-of-fact. Of course, she told herself, this was nothing new to him. She might even ask him, *And you aren't planning to kill me?* But she didn't.

"I won't ask for your help," he told her. "You get him in the house, and that's the last I'll ask. But it might help *you* to remind yourself that he's not just a danger to vampires; he's so intent on getting at us that he's a danger to your kind, too. No matter what, keep reminding yourself of that school bus tumbling into the ditch."

"All right," she said.

"Plus your father, your brother, *anybody* who gets in his way."

"*All right*," she repeated more emphatically. "I'll do it. It's not a very good plan, you know. Too many loopholes, too many places where he might not believe me, where things might go wrong."

Ethan spread his hands in an I'm-open-to-suggestions gesture.

She didn't have any.

He watched her intently, gauging, not liking—she was sure—that his life would be in her hands. There *must* be other vampires, Kerry thought. If he didn't have to protect *them*, surely Ethan would just move on—to a different identity, in a different place. As he'd obviously had experience doing before. But finally he nodded. He handed her the keys to the new Monte Carlo. "Then it begins," he said. "And, Kerry, need I mention? If you can't have him back here by six-thirty, don't bring him at all."

"Sunrise isn't until after seven."

"If you aren't here by six-thirty," he repeated, "I won't be either. Which means if you bring him here *after* six-thirty—"

"I'll be on my own," she finished for him. So he didn't trust her, not completely. "How about," she suggested, "if I don't find him by six, I'll come back here alone and we can look again tomorrow?"

He considered, then inclined his head in agreement. "Fine."

"What if I find him but he won't come until after sunrise?"

Ethan smiled at her. "Then I hope you can come up with a convincing reason for him why I'm not here. And"—again he threw her own words back at her—"you will be on your own. And so will your father and brother. Vampires are by nature a conservative and cautious lot. Unlike the young, we know exactly how much we have to lose. You don't want me nervous about your intentions."

"You don't need to threaten me," she said.

He just sat there looking at her, with his eyes cool and distant, an unspoken reminder that—should he decide she'd let him down—he had all the time in the world to plot revenge.

CHAPTER SIXTEEN

K ERRY RECOGNIZED THE first flaw in the plan as soon as she pulled the Monte Carlo away from the curb. There was no way she could go to the supermarket to see if Professor Marsala was there because that was the one place she was bound to be recognized.

Doesn't matter, she told herself. Surely if the professor planned to spend the greater part of the night in one place, it wouldn't be there, where somebody was sure to notice after the first two or three hours that he was lurking in the frozen-foods aisle. Restaurants and bars made much more sense.

The first place she looked was the Student Union at the college, since that was the place where the professor was most likely to find people he knew, people who were most apt to intervene if strangers with long, sharp teeth tried to drag him out. The place was incredibly noisy, with music and talking and a whole crowd of people out to have a good time on a Saturday night. It also wasn't very well lit, so that Kerry had to wander in among the tables, staring. No sign of the man whose picture she'd seen on the piano.

Next she started going to the restaurants. "I'm supposed to be meeting someone," she'd tell the host or hostess. "May I look to see if he's here yet?"

He never was.

The bars were worse. When she went into the first one, the bartender called out to her, "Proof."

"Excuse me?" Kerry wasn't trying to order something— all she'd done was walk into the place. Maybe she hadn't heard right. She had the impression everyone was staring at her, thinking how dumb she was.

"Proof of age," the bartender said. "Got to be twenty-one to be legal in New York State."

"I'm not twenty-one," Kerry stammered.

"No kidding. You can't be in here, then."

"I'm looking for"—she realized what it would sound like if she said *someone*—"my father."

"He's not here," the bartender said. "Please leave before I have to have you escorted out."

"How do you know he's not here?" she demanded.

"No fatherly types at all." The bartender signaled to someone, and Kerry said, "I'm going, I'm going."

She turned around in the doorway for a last look. No sign of Marsala, but the bouncer that the bartender had summoned was closing in fast.

Kerry left. Even if the professor *was* there, he'd have to

leave eventually—she checked her watch—*soon*, before the place shut down for the night.

The second bar was bad, too, though in a different way.

A woman—she must have been the manager—came bustling over as soon as Kerry stepped across the threshold. "I'm looking for my father," Kerry said before the woman could start in on her. "Please." She heard the desperation in her voice, and apparently the manager did, too.

Her face softened. "Oh, you poor dearie," she said.

Kerry tried to look more like a poor dearie.

The woman escorted her from room to room—the place was a converted house—and even offered to call the police for her.

"No, no," Kerry said. "Don't bother. He always comes home eventually."

The woman patted her hand sympathetically and said, "Oh, you poor dearie," again.

Kerry even checked the other supermarket, the one where she didn't work. Not likely, she knew, but it was only two o'clock, which gave her another four and a half hours.

After that, she drove back to the college and started all over again. Her search was shorter this time, since several of the places had closed, and in those places that were still open there was less of a crowd.

The third time she went to the Student Union she found him.

About twenty people were left from the night's earlier crowd, spread out in two main groups; one was clustered around a TV set, watching *The Attack of the Killer Tomatoes;* those in the smaller group were arguing because they wanted to start an alternative campus newspaper but couldn't agree on a name for it. A lone girl was reciting sad poetry about bad men, accompanying herself on guitar; and a couple sat holding hands, the girl crying, the boy speaking softly but earnestly. The cashier, who looked like a student himself, sat on a stool, smoking despite the NO SMOKING sign and playing some sort of hand-held electronic game that sporadically beeped or played music.

Seated in what Kerry would have been willing to bet was the exact center of the room was Professor Gilbert Marsala. He was thinner than he'd been at the time the picture was taken, his hairline farther back, but there was never any doubt in her mind who it was. He was drinking from a mug and reading a book, though he looked up every few seconds, glancing all around nervously. He spotted Kerry as soon as she started toward him, and she saw his gaze flick around the room as he tried to decide who best to approach for help.

She held her hands out—fronts, then backs—to demonstrate she carried no weapons, and she gestured behind her, which was meant to draw his attention to the fact that she was alone.

Marsala looked tense, but at least he didn't bolt.

"I'm all alone," Kerry said as soon as she was within range and could say it softly, so as not to attract attention. "Please, can we talk? Here is fine." He didn't look like she'd expected. Somehow she'd thought he'd have a twitch, or some manic gleam in his eye, something that would mark him as a man with inner demons. Someone fanatic enough to run over anyone who got in his way and steal people's fathers and little boys from their homes.

Kerry sat down, placing her hands on the table where he could see them. "Where are my father and brother?" she asked.

"I don't know." For a second she thought he was going

170

to deny knowing what she was talking about, but then he added, "Home by now, I guess. Or still in the hospital. Or maybe the police have them. I let them go, you know."

She'd seen they weren't home and she wasn't sure whether to believe the other possibilities, but any note of hope was good to hear anyway. "I'm not a vampire," she said. She could see the thought *Sure, you're not* travel through his brain. "Any test," she assured him, "*any*thing you can think of, I'll do it."

He sat looking at her. "You were with them."

"Yes." There was certainly no use denying it. "Regina and Ethan. I never met them before Thursday night. I didn't know what they were."

"They killed my friends—Phil and George, Ken, Danny, and Marcia."

"I know," she said. That sounded worse than it was. "I mean, I didn't know until after."

"I was watching," Marsala said, and for an awful moment she thought he meant he'd seen his friends die. "I saw him drive up with you, introduce you to her." And she realized he must have been somewhere near Ethan's house. "I saw him clean the blood out of the car, and then I saw them drive you home. Like a damned escort service."

"It was his blood," Kerry said, not sure how Marsala was interpreting what he'd seen. Did he think Ethan had fed on her in her father's car, making her a vampire that very night, or that it was Marsala's friends' blood and that she had helped kill them? "*Ethan's* blood. His own. Your friends were going to kill him. I came into it in the middle of things. I didn't understand. I thought they were crazy and they were going to kill some poor innocent guy."

"He's no innocent," Marsala said.

"I know that now." Kerry nodded for emphasis. She

couldn't bring herself to say any of the things Ethan had suggested. She just said, "I do know it."

"Did they drink your blood?" He reached to push the loose strands of hair away from her neck but stopped, perhaps thinking touching her was inappropriate, or maybe realizing the marks would have gone away by now in any case.

She swept the hair clear anyway. "No," she said firmly.

"She drank Joey's blood."

There was no answer for that.

"I watched him change into one of them."

Kerry wasn't sure she'd heard that right. "You . . . *watched . . . ?"*

"It took a while. Four, five months from the time he first met her."

"No," Kerry said, but before she could explain that it only took seconds, he continued, "At first we didn't know. There were all those rehearsals, twice a week, then three times; every night by the last two weeks. Ridiculous schedule for a school production, like the play was more important than the school-work. But then it was finally over. Except that it wasn't over. 'I'm going out,' he said. Every night. Just like that. 'I'm going out.' He led us to believe it was one of the girls from the play, but then Patty, my wife, and I found out it was that Regina woman, the director. 'She's older than *I* am,' Patty said. He didn't care. She'd bitten him by then."

"I'm not sure what you're saying," Kerry admitted.

"She encouraged him to lie to us. She taught him to smoke marijuana, and she provided him with liquor even though he was underage. He'd never done any of those things before. His marks . . . He'd been a straight-A student in high school, dean's list every semester. But suddenly he was failing and taking incompletes. Dropped his old friends, dropped his old

172

interests. Stayed up all night, partying, didn't want to get up in the morning. Talked back to his mother, sassed me. We had no idea then, but it was the vampire's bite. He was changing into one of them right before our very eyes, and we didn't know it. Then I started following her. Then I saw."

Kerry shook her head. "That's not—"

Marsala pointed a finger at her. "I didn't know how to stop it." He nodded slowly. "I do now."

He'd stopped it with Regina.

"Professor Marsala," Kerry said. She didn't dare say, *Your son was growing up and he made bad decisions,* or *That's called rebellion, not vampirism.* His story was an awful mishmash combining truth and speculation and, she supposed, a father's grief and guilt. She said, "It isn't like that. Either someone's a vampire or not; it doesn't take months."

"That what one of them told you?"

She nodded.

"Do you believe everything they tell you?"

"No," she said. "Of course not. But—"

"Don't believe anything," Marsala said. "I don't know what they promised him. But then, when they'd strung him out long enough, when they were done laughing at him, they killed him. The police thought it was a car accident."

She remembered Ethan saying that he and Regina had arranged the deaths of Marsala's friends to look like part of a struggle between opposing drug factions. Of course they wouldn't discard drained bodies carelessly. The vampires couldn't afford to have people speculating in that direction. And as Ethan had admitted, unexplained disappearances raised too many questions.

Marsala was nodding, as though to encourage her to believe. "He'd been drinking. Car hit a tree. But I knew. That woman was evil. She turned our son against us. I started tracking her, and I found out what she was; then I kept on tracking her because I knew there couldn't be just one. 'Wait long enough and she'll lead us to more,' I said. Even Patty didn't believe me. She couldn't face it and she ran away. But I knew. The sunlight proved me right."

An image of what had been left of Regina flashed through her mind. Although she wasn't aware of it, it must have shown on her face, for Marsala said, "You saw her? You saw what the sunlight did? Don't feel sorry for her. Do you know why sunlight destroys them?"

Kerry shook her head.

"Because God won't permit such evil to exist under the sun."

Kerry bit her lip to keep from asking why, then, God would permit such evil to exist under the moon.

"You"—Marsala pointed at her again—"you're an in-between case. Like Joey. Seduced by the glamor of evil."

The word *seduced* made her cheeks grow warm, which he no doubt saw.

He nodded, and she was sure he thought it was worse than it was. "Fight them," he said. "I know they've got their claws in you, but fight them."

"They *do not* have their claws in me," Kerry protested, "and at least they don't go around ramming school buses and kidnapping innocent people."

"I don't think you know half of what they do," Marsala said. Which was probably true. "How old is your young-looking friend? Fifty years? A hundred? Two hundred? Multiply that times three hundred sixty-five nights a year, and call *me* cold blooded."

"They don't kill every night."

"Something else they told you?"

Ethan hadn't killed last night, she thought. Or, at least, she was fairly certain he hadn't. On the other hand, the night before, he and Regina had killed four. And tonight he was planning on killing at least one.

She ran her hand through her hair. "I don't want to argue," she said. "I didn't come here to defend them. But I'm not one of them. And I'm not one-of-them-in-training. I want some assurance that you haven't hurt my dad and my brother. If you can give me that, I'll tell you where Ethan is, and how you can get him."

Marsala sat back and looked at her as though evaluating. "Vampires don't lie?" he asked.

"I never said that. I just—"

"Do you lie?"

Kerry worked hard to look him right in the eyes. "No."

"Then you told your father exactly what happened Thursday night."

Kerry looked away. "I . . . He didn't ask, and I didn't volunteer the information."

"Which is not the same as lying?" Marsala said.

There was no good answer to that.

"Then let me ask you this," Marsala continued. "How did your friend know who I was?"

"He recognized your picture in the paper."

"If he saw the paper"—Marsala gave a grim smile—"how is it you didn't know your father and your brother are safe?"

"What?"

"You didn't ask, and he didn't volunteer the information?"

"I don't understand what you're getting at."

"They were in the car," Marsala said. "In the trunk. If they're not home now, the police must have them in protective custody."

"You—" Kerry made a conscious effort to lower her voice. "You rammed into a school bus with my father and brother in the trunk of the car? You could have killed them. They could have suffocated."

"I admit I wasn't thinking straight," Marsala said. "I went to your house to get you. When I found you weren't home from school yet, I forced your family to get into the car, with no clear plan in mind. When I saw the bus . . . It was stupid, I admit. I didn't think of those other children on the bus. I only thought of you, becoming what I had seen Joey becoming, feeding on people's blood, killing people, night after night after night for centuries. I didn't stop to think—about your family in the back *or* about your innocent classmates. But my point is, unlike the vampires, *I* didn't hurt anyone. The people on the school bus survived, and your family survived." Marsala waggled his finger at her. "And your friend didn't tell you that. He figured he could use you better if you didn't know."

"He didn't know," Kerry started, then she changed that to "*I* don't know. You might have them buried in a shallow grave in your backyard, for all I know."

Marsala turned around in his seat and called out to the student cashier, "Max!"

"Yo," Max said, not quite diverting his attention from his game.

"Do you still have that newspaper? The one with the picture you thought looked like me?"

Max rapidly hit a few more buttons before reaching under the counter. He tossed the newspaper, and it almost made it to their table.

Marsala leaned over and picked it up, then folded it back to the front page. There was her school picture, and the diagram of the accident scene, and the composite drawing of Marsala. The professor tapped his finger on a paragraph in the first column. ". . . Stephen and Ian Nowicki," the article said, "found tied and gagged in the trunk of the car, shaken but unharmed." The following paragraphs described how a man wearing a ski mask and armed with a gun had forced his way into their house, demanding to know where sixteen-year-old Kerry Nowicki was. Told she was still at school, he'd tied them and gagged them. Then, after searching the house, he trashed the living room, after which he forced them into the trunk of their own car.

The article said that Stephen Nowicki felt the car swerve and hit something repeatedly, but at some point during the crash into the bus or the fire hydrant, he banged his head on the car's tire iron and lost consciousness. During the time the police and ambulance were at the scene, only four-year-old Ian Nowicki was conscious, and he had been warned by the intruder not to make a sound, "or else." So he dutifully remained quiet. By the time his father regained consciousness, the car had apparently been impounded by the police because no one heard his cries for help. The two weren't discovered until police investigating the bus incident opened the trunk at about nine o'clock in the evening.

Kerry looked up from the newspaper and met Marsala's triumphant smile. "He knew," she whispered.

"Apparently he didn't think it was important enough to mention," Marsala said.

Kerry couldn't think of how often they'd skirted the subject of her family this evening. Ethan knew how frightened she was for them. Over and over he'd had the chance to say, *They're all right. Marsala doesn't have them.* Relief and a sense of betrayal balanced so precariously she didn't know whether to laugh out loud or cry.

"They're treacherous," Marsala said. "You can't trust them. They don't think like we do. They don't even consider themselves human. They're like aliens; they're like vile and vicious animals." Marsala reached out and covered her hand with his. It was warm and slightly rough, as though chapped from the weather or from honest work. "Will you really help me stop him from killing other people's sons and daughters?" he asked. "Or are you here to defend him?"

"He knew," Kerry repeated. "I held my little brother's toy bear and cried, thinking he and my father might both be dead. And Ethan didn't say anything. I cried in front of him, and he didn't say anything."

She looked into Marsala's face, the face of a man who'd lost his son and—in a different way—his wife to vampires. A man who'd been unable for three years to convince anyone of the terrible truth only he knew, and who'd fought back in the only way he could.

"He wanted me to trick you," she said, "to convince you that I was helping you, but to bring you back to his house, where he planned to kill you."

"Good," Marsala said.

"*Good?*"

He had a quirky smile that reminded her of the picture she'd seen of his son, Joe. "I don't mean *good* that he plans to kill me; I mean *good* that you told me. We've had enough lies told to us, I think, you and me. So I'll tell you the truth, Kerry Nowicki: No matter how good a little helper you've been to this vampire, he can't afford to let you live. You have to decide who's going to die: him—or you and me."

CHAPTER SEVENTEEN

KERRY TOLD MARSALA everything she'd learned about Ethan. Some of it he didn't believe, and she couldn't tell if that was because he thought she was lying or because he thought Ethan had lied to her. By the end she wasn't sure how much of it she herself believed.

"Do you know how he plans to kill me?" Marsala asked.

"No," Kerry said.

"But you do accept that he plans to?"

"He admitted it." Kerry squirmed because by saying so, she admitted that she had knowingly plotted to kill the man she now was facing.

Marsala didn't point that out. Instead he said, "Pull your chair around closer."

Kerry glanced around to see if somebody appeared to be listening. The young couple in the back looked cheerier— they were sharing an order of french fries—but other than that everybody in the room looked the same as when she'd entered. She moved her chair closer to Marsala anyway.

He reached into the inner pocket of his jacket. "Don't get jumpy," he warned.

And, by that, she knew.

He didn't pull the gun out of his pocket; he was just showing her. "I don't suppose," he said, not sounding very hopeful, "you've ever used one?"

Kerry shook her head. "What good's a gun going to be against a vampire anyway?"

"Fired from close enough, this'll slow him down."

Kerry remembered the laundry, remembered Sidowski holding his revolver up to Ethan's head and saying much the same thing. She forced the image from her mind.

"They heal fast, but not that fast. Besides, this has silver bullets."

"Isn't that for werewolves?" Kerry asked, eager to stop thinking, to lose herself in the details.

By the disgusted look on Marsala's face, she guessed that whoever had sold him the gun and ammunition must have said something similar.

"Vampires can't stand the touch of silver," Marsala said. "Same as garlic. Not as bad as sunlight, but it'll be an extra kick."

Kick, she thought.

Kerry wondered if that was just another superstition, like that vampires' images aren't reflected in mirrors, which she had seen wasn't true. Ethan hadn't mentioned anything about silver; but, then again, if it *was* true, Kerry supposed he wouldn't have.

If it was true, maybe it would serve to kill him more quickly, painlessly.

Marsala said, "I want you to take this and hide it. See if you've got a pocket big enough. Otherwise you can stick it in the waistband of your jeans."

"I'm not sticking a gun down my pants," Kerry whispered at him.

"It's got a safety," Marsala said. "Check your pockets."

They weren't *her* pockets. It was Ethan's jacket, which seemed terribly unfair. There *was* an inner pocket. "I can't," she said. "I could never shoot anybody."

"Not even knowing what he is?" Marsala asked. "Not even knowing he's killed uncountable others, and intends to kill you, and may well decide that your family has seen too much and kill them, too?"

Kerry withered under this onslaught. "I don't know," she admitted. "But even if I wanted to, I'm sure I'd never be able to hit him. I have terrible aim when it comes to—"

Marsala had taken the gun out of his pocket and was holding it under the table. "Take the damn gun before somebody sees it," he interrupted. "All I'm asking is for you to hold it."

Kerry took the gun. The dark metal was cold, and it was heavier than she would have thought. She gingerly stuck it into her pocket.

"Here's an extra clip." Marsala handed over the extra bullets. "Put it into the outside pocket, same side."

"Why?" Kerry asked.

"Same side so that it's easy to find. Outside pocket so that when you pull out the gun, you don't pull out the clip at the same time and drop it."

Not only did it make sense, it almost sounded as though he knew her.

"In case you *do* need to use it"—Kerry shook her head, but he kept on talking—"you need to slide back the safety by the trigger. Stop shaking your head and listen. It can't hurt to know."

He was right. Kerry stopped shaking her head.

"The safety," he repeated, "is by the trigger. You push it back with your thumb. *If* you fire, it'll recoil—it'll kick back. So be prepared for that. The empty shell will drop out automatically and the next bullet will be ready to fire. You don't need to release the safety again, but you need to let go of the trigger, then pull it back for the second shot. Do you understand?"

"More or less," Kerry said miserably.

"Do you understand?" Marsala insisted.

"Yes."

"The clip holds nine bullets. We're not even going to talk about reloading."

Good, Kerry thought, but she knew not to say it.

Marsala put his hand over hers again. She didn't like it, but pulling away seemed too unfriendly a gesture.

"I know this is difficult for you," he said. "But if he manages to take me by surprise, he'd be a fool not to search me for weapons. And one thing this vampire isn't is a fool."

"I understand." Kerry wriggled her hand free and pushed her hair back from her forehead, then she put both hands in her lap.

"Just be ready to hand it to me," Marsala said. "And I

probably *will say* 'it,' rather than 'gun,' which might or might not give us another second or so of surprise. Whatever you do, don't let him separate us."

"All right."

Then, before Kerry was ready for it, Marsala stood. "We might as well get started. The closer we get to his cutoff time, the more nervous he's going to get, the more eager he's going to be to do it fast—which gives us less of a chance to turn the tables on him. Steady now." He took her elbow to help her get to her feet. "It's more clear cut than you think. It's good versus evil no matter how attractively the evil disguises itself."

"Fine," Kerry said. He was right, she knew he was right: Did he have to be so self-righteous about it?

"Just don't let him confuse you," Marsala warned.

THE STUDENT UNION was situated in the middle of the campus, easy access for those who lived and went to school in the surrounding buildings, which meant that there were no parking lots right nearby. Which meant that Marsala could have parked in any of several places.

Which meant that Ethan must have been following her all along and been waiting for them, even though Kerry hadn't heard a thing, hadn't seen a thing.

Because, suddenly, he was there, materializing out of the shadows as Marsala leaned to unlock the car door, his arm crossing in front of Marsala so that his open palm rested against Marsala's chin, the other hand placed behind the professor's neck.

The fact that he obviously hadn't trusted her, combined with the fact that she had just betrayed him, served to bring the color to her cheeks. Was his eyesight good enough to be able to tell?

"I could kill you here and now," Ethan warned Marsala, "though in principle I'm against leaving dead bodies strewn about parking lots."

Kerry saw Marsala's eyes shift to her, but he didn't say anything, and he didn't struggle. Ethan, standing behind, had no way to see. He kept one hand under Marsala's chin but ran the other along Marsala's torso. Kerry could tell he found something by the way he reached into one of Marsala's pockets.

A second gun? Kerry wondered. Didn't Marsala trust her either?

But what Ethan pulled out was something much smaller, and not at all shiny. It took her several seconds, and then it was the smell that told her: a handful of garlic cloves.

With an expression of mild disgust, which may have been for nothing more than the smell, Ethan let them drop. "Get in the backseat," he ordered. "Kerry, you drive."

Marsala handed her the keys. She couldn't tell from his face what he wanted her to do.

Ethan got in the back with him.

What was she supposed to do if Ethan attacked him there, drinking his blood while she was behind the wheel? Marsala's gun weighted down the jacket, so it hung lower on the right-hand side.

"Ethan?" Could he hear the tremor in her voice? Would it make him suspicious?

"His house," Ethan said.

It would help if she could read his expression. When Marsala was talking, she could recognize his emotions: hate for the vampires, tenderness for his son, anticipation mixed with fear at the thought of having this finally done. But she couldn't tell what Ethan was feeling, whether it was anger at Regina's killer, or satisfaction because he'd caught him, or simple bloodlust.

What should I do? she wondered.

Sitting behind the steering wheel, it took Kerry several seconds to realize she couldn't follow Ethan's instructions, even if she wanted to. "It's a stick shift," she said. "I don—"

"Push in the clutch with your left foot," Ethan told her, "then turn the key."

Nothing happened.

"Do it again," Ethan instructed. "Keep the clutch in."

This time the car started.

"All right, put the car in gear: pull the stick toward your leg, then straight back. There's a diagram on the ball. You want to go from P to one."

Kerry did exactly what Ethan said, and nothing happened. She pressed harder on the accelerator, and the engine raced, but still the car didn't move.

"Ease up on the clutch," Ethan said. "Slowly."

The car shudder-hopped several feet.

"More gas," Ethan advised.

The car lurched forward and Kerry slammed on the brake. The engine stalled. "I hate this," she said.

"Try again."

The fourth or fifth time the car stalled, Ethan finally gave up.

"All right," he said. "Kerry, you get in the back. We'll ride in front."

She'd been afraid that he would abandon her there in the parking lot, which would leave Marsala weaponless and on his own. But the fact that he wanted her along strengthened Marsala's claim that Ethan planned to kill her, too, once he'd gotten rid of Marsala.

Ethan pulled Marsala out of the car. He opened the front passenger door, obviously intent on getting in first and then pulling Marsala in after him, which would entail crawling over the stick shift—but that way at least Marsala wouldn't be alone in the front seat. However, taking up the entire passenger seat was a toolbox, the huge kind, such as Kerry would have imagined a professional construction worker having.

"I'll move it," Kerry offered. She'd gotten out of the driver's seat and circled around to the right side of the car, but Ethan—still holding on to Marsala with his right hand—had already leaned in to get it out of the way himself.

Kerry saw him freeze, then turn to Marsala. She looked over his outstretched arm. At first she couldn't tell what had happened, except that the cover had come up. Then she realized what was in the box: at least a half dozen pointed, two-foot-long stakes, a mallet, a silver crucifix, and—by the smell—more garlic at the bottom. On top of it all was a hatchet, no doubt the one Marsala had used on Regina.

Seeing the hatchet, imagining Marsala watching Regina die in the sunlight and then chopping off her head, Kerry felt her resolve begin to melt. She glanced at Ethan, expecting to see anguish or—at the very least—fury. *Nothing*. She could read nothing on his face.

"Take the box in back, would you, Kerry?" he asked in a perfectly level, perfectly calm voice.

Kerry closed the cover and picked up the box, which was heavy but manageable. She stepped out of the way to let Ethan enter. Then—at the moment Ethan was occupied with dragging Marsala in after him—she turned, holding out her coat in a gesture that was an unwelcome reminder of the Rochester prostitutes. She felt the tug as Marsala took the gun from her inner pocket. By the time Ethan was settled behind the steering wheel, Marsala, next to him, had the gun in his own pocket, and Kerry was sitting in the backseat with Marsala's vampire-hunting kit.

CHAPTER EIGHTEEN

E THAN KEPT A wary watch on Marsala as he drove, no
doubt ready to grab him if he tried to escape from the
car, to shove him back if he lunged.

Marsala, of course, did neither; and Kerry, hunched miserably in the backseat, realized she was too confused to actively hope for anything.

Except that she could keep from crying.

Which, the moment she thought about it, she couldn't.

She bit her lip, trying to regain control, sure—at least—
she was being so quiet no one would notice.

"Kerry?" Ethan, spreading his attention between Marsala
and driving, spared a quick glance in her direction. Then
another. "Did he hurt you?" Before she could answer, he

grabbed a handful of Marsala's jacket and shoved him so that his head bounced off the side window, saying, "If you hurt her—"

"No!" Kerry said at the same time Marsala said the same thing. "I'm all right," she insisted.

She could see Ethan's skeptical reflection in the rearview mirror. He kept hold of Marsala until he had to downshift, and even then he let go reluctantly.

And what was she supposed to make of that? She rested her forehead in her hand and didn't move until Ethan pulled the car into Marsala's driveway.

"Out," he told Marsala, and he began sliding him across the seat and out the door. To Kerry he said, "Stay here."

"No." Surely when Marsala had told her not to let Ethan separate them, he had been more afraid of getting separated from his gun than from her, but she couldn't just abandon him now. Marsala *was* on the side of right, she told herself as Ethan's blue eyes, surprised, turned in her direction. *Remember Regina's house,* she told herself. *Remember Bergen Swamp.* "If anybody looks out and sees me just sitting here, they'll get suspicious," she explained.

"All right, then," Ethan said in a tone that was like an icicle melting down her jacket collar. "In that case, you can carry the box."

Did he guess she'd betrayed him? Had she just failed his final test by not admitting it and begging his forgiveness? *Don't be silly,* she told herself. If Ethan suspected her, she couldn't imagine he'd waste time and effort with tests.

They used Marsala's key this time and turned on the light that hung over the entryway stairwell.

"Up," Ethan ordered.

Kerry followed the two of them.

"You like the idea of drinking my blood in my own house, vampire?" Marsala asked. "That's what the other one, the female, would have done, too. I tracked her. I followed her for two years before she led me to you, and I got to know her habits. She had a great sense of irony."

At the head of the stairs, Ethan gave him a shove into the living room.

"Or are you going to let the girl drain me? Is that how the transition is made, with the first kill?"

Kerry set the vampire-hunter's box down at the top of the stairs, wondering if he was just stalling for time or whether he really believed that, as though the fact that she had helped him wasn't enough to convince him Ethan had never bitten her.

"Nobody's going to feed on you," Ethan said. He backed Marsala up against the wall, holding him by the shoulders so that Marsala couldn't get to the gun.

Why didn't he do it before? Kerry thought. *In the car, in the driveway, going up the stairs?* Not that she wanted to see Ethan killed, but she knew there was no other way.

"I see," Marsala said. How could he remain so cool? Didn't he know how quickly Ethan could move? "We're just here because we're all good friends," Marsala said.

"We're just here to make your death look like something else," Ethan corrected. He tossed a set of keys onto the coffee table. Kerry could see the Ferrari symbol: Regina's keys, to give the police a lead in her disappearance, even if the body was never found.

"What's the matter?" Marsala taunted. "Don't you want to do it in front of the girl? Don't you want her to see you with my blood dripping off your fangs, smeared on your teeth and chin? Don't you want her to see what you are before you finish making her one of you?" He didn't wait for an answer. "Kerry"—she jumped at the suddenness of his calling her name—"there's a tape recorder in the box, under the stakes. Get it out and press PLAY."

Ethan gave her a confused and worried glance.

He hadn't known, Kerry saw. He hadn't guessed. He hadn't suspected. The thought had never crossed his mind.

But it did now.

"Do it," Marsala commanded.

"No." Ethan didn't know what was going on—*Kerry* couldn't tell what Marsala planned—but he definitely needed to see which of them she'd listen to.

"I'm sorry," Kerry said. She opened the box and lifted the tray out, exposing a portable AM/FM radio–tape player and the garlic she'd suspected all along.

"Kerry," Ethan said uncertainly, spending a dangerous amount of attention on her.

Kerry pressed the PLAY button.

There was the hiss of the tape before the recording started, and Marsala said, "And now take out the gun."

She jerked her head up. She had an instant of terror, supposing a second gun that she couldn't find, before she saw both men start to move. There was no gun. But with no way to know that, Ethan released Marsala and lunged toward Kerry.

While Marsala went for the gun in his pocket.

Kerry, still on the staircase, dropped to her knees and covered her head, knowing what woefully inadequate protection that would be against vampires or bullets.

There were two shots, and Ethan cried out in pain, just as the music on the recorder started—loud classical music, perhaps the overture to an opera, just the kind of music to camouflage murder.

Kerry forced herself to look up.

She had been sure Marsala would aim for the head to inflict the worst damage. She was sure that she would look up to find Ethan dead or dying, but Marsala had shot him in the leg. The left leg, she noted irrelevantly, the leg opposite from the one that had been injured last time. Both bullets had hit him in the thigh. As Ethan tried to sit up, Marsala came closer and fired a third bullet into his right knee.

Kerry covered her mouth to keep from crying out.

Ethan doubled over, not making a sound this time. Marsala had a clear shot at his head if that was what he intended.

But apparently that wasn't what he intended.

"You," he said, motioning to Kerry.

She had to pass by Ethan, who watched her but made no move to stop her.

She remembered him saying that vampires didn't feel hot or cold the way humans did, and she told herself that he couldn't feel pain to the same extent that a human would, either. As proof, she pointed out to herself that otherwise he would have screamed when Marsala's third bullet hit his knee. Surely his first outcry had been from startlement. She remembered how hurt and scared he had looked in the laundry, and how that had been an act.

"I'm sorry," she said again.

"Open the drapes," Marsala told her.

She glanced at Ethan, who was looking from her to Marsala.

"Do I have to say everything twice?" Marsala demanded.

Kerry knelt on the couch to reach the cord that opened the drapes covering the picture window.

"The side window, too. And the sliding-glass door in the kitchen. That's the main one. It faces east." Marsala checked his watch, then glanced at the tape recorder. "Come . . . oh, long before Madame Butterfly realizes she's been betrayed, the sun is going to rise up over those trees and flood this whole part of the house with all that lovely, cleansing light. How long since you've seen a sunrise, vampire?"

Ethan met his smirk levelly and said nothing.

Kerry crossed in front of him again to go into the kitchen, to open the drapes over the door that led from the kitchen to a small wooden deck in back of the house. *Stop it*, she wished at Marsala. There was no need to gloat and torment Ethan. She remembered, again, how Ethan had almost killed her at Regina's house. *"I'm not going to hurt you,"* he'd promised. She tried to replace that image with the one from Bergen Swamp, when he'd been angry, but then he'd only kissed her neck. As in: *Tag, you're it.* So maybe he hadn't been angry after all. That one was too hard to figure out. Once again the thought of Regina's house forced itself into her mind. He'd held her slightly off to the side, so that she'd been pressed against his chest, but that was all, as though he was taking into account her age and lack of experience, or the fact that she'd helped him the night before.

"Oh, you're quiet now," Marsala said to Ethan. "But we're going to need Madame Butterfly to cover your screams later."

"Professor Marsala," she begged.

"I take it," Marsala continued as though she hadn't spoken, "circumstances being what they are, that neither of you has ever witnessed a vampire's death by sunlight."

Ethan briefly closed his eyes, then opened them again as though to say he could face whatever Marsala had to say.

"Let me share my experience," Marsala said. He had to

194

raise his voice because, on the tape, singers had now joined the orchestra. "I entered the female vampire's house at about noon. I expected that I would find her asleep in a coffin in the basement. Imagine my surprise when I found her in an elegantly decorated bedroom, wearing a modest though alluring negligee, probably purchased at Kaufmann's or Lord and Taylor. Not the Halloween scene I expected at all. Still, I set my kit down." He indicated the box by the steps. "I arranged the stakes on the floor so she could see them when she awoke, turned on *Madame Butterfly* to allay the fears of neighbors who might otherwise be concerned by any unaccustomed noise, laid the crucifix down on her bosom, then gently opened the vampire's mouth and placed several cloves of garlic inside. She stirred just the faintest bit then, but she didn't awake. And then I opened the windows."

What have I done? Kerry thought, seeing the relish with which he told his story.

"First I pulled back the drapes. There were two sets of windows. I opened the drapes of one, then the other. She frowned, in her sleep. I could see the little line, here"—he indicated between the eyebrows—"as though she might have been having a bad dream. Perhaps remembering a victim's blood that didn't taste as sweet as she had anticipated." Marsala smiled into Ethan's look of loathing. "And then I pulled open the shutters. First one"—he gave a flourish with his hand—"and then the other. Of course, she started screaming as soon as the first was open."

Ethan closed his eyes again.

"Well," Marsala corrected himself, "she didn't actually *scream* at first, because there was all that garlic in her mouth. But she was spitting out the garlic and making these noises deep in her throat that would have been screams if she could have gotten them out, and she thrashed on the bed, but she couldn't get up. Because of the crucifix. Her skin became red . . . oh, in seconds. She went from seriously sunburned to raw and blistered in the time it took her to realize what was happening and to clear the garlic from her mouth. She begged for mercy. Not for me to let her live—she knew it was too late for that—but for me to use the stakes or the hatchet on her. Do your victims ever beg for mercy, vampire? Did Joey? Don't"—Marsala made a gesture as though to cut Ethan off, though Ethan hadn't given any indication he was going to speak—"don't tell me you weren't the one to kill Joey. I know you weren't even in Brockport then. But surely you vampires discuss such things, don't you? 'Oh, I had such an interesting dinner the other night. First I won his trust, and then I ripped his throat out. My God, he screamed won-derfully.' Do you share vampire stories like that?"

Ethan didn't answer.

This isn't necessary, Kerry wanted to shout at Marsala. *You don't need to do this.*

Marsala asked, "Or is one just the same as any other for you? She didn't ever mention him, did she? She probably couldn't even remember his name by the next morning, could she?" His fingers flexed on his gun.

Kerry braced herself for the shot she was sure was coming, but Marsala gave another smile.

"You can't goad me," he said. "You don't get off that easy." He took a deep breath. "So, she may not have known what I meant when I kept repeating, 'I'm Joe's father.'" He shrugged. "But I was everyone's father at that moment. I stood there for everyone she'd killed over the years. I watched her skin blacken. And crack. And curl. And fall off. Did I mention the smell of burnt meat? Finally, the little gurgling noises coming from her throat stopped. And a while after that the body stopped twitching. That was when I chopped off her head, to make sure she couldn't come back. There was hardly any blood by then. What there was, on the edge of my blade, boiled away in the sunlight. Then I closed the shutters and the drapes, so that the house would look the same as always. I rewound *Madame Butterfly*. We hadn't even got very far into it. Five, six minutes at the very most. I'm sure it seemed much longer for her." Marsala looked at Ethan appraisingly. "I imagine you'll take longer to die, with the weaker early morning sunlight."

"Professor Marsala," Kerry said, "why are you doing this?"

"I want the names of other vampires," Marsala said.

It was, she could see, what Ethan had expected.

"I was too eager to see the female vampire die," Marsala said.

"Regina," Kerry corrected, fed up with this. "Her name was Regina." Which it may or may not have been, after all these years. "Professor Marsala, you can't do this. It's one thing to kill them to protect yourself, but you have no right to torture—"

"I was too eager to see the female vampire die," Marsala insisted to Ethan. "The last thing I should have done was fill her mouth so that she couldn't talk. You *will* talk. And if you talk fast enough and if I believe what you're saying, I may give you one of the easier deaths she begged for." Marsala checked his watch. "Not a lot of time to make up your mind," he announced cheerfully. "Although no doubt you have an inner sense that's already told you that. . . . And perhaps I shouldn't have used the crucifix to hold her down, so that she could have thrashed even more."

Beyond the look of pure hate Ethan was wearing, there was a flicker of contempt.

Marsala saw it; Kerry knew he did. He smiled smugly as he walked past Ethan, leaving a wide clearance around the wounded vampire as he approached the toolbox where he kept his supplies. He set the safety on his gun and tucked it into his belt. "Let's see. If you *do* cooperate, which of these would you prefer I use? Understand, we won't have a lot of time for decisions at that point." He touched the point of one of the stakes to show that the pun was intentional. "And you probably won't be very coherent by then, spitting up your own blood and all. One of these? Or this?" His hand strayed to the hatchet. "Or this?" He picked up the silver crucifix and held it triumphantly in Ethan's direction.

If he was expecting Ethan to cringe, he must have been disappointed. Ethan looked close to laughing. Which may or may not have been budding hysteria. But still he said nothing, which Marsala obviously found infuriating.

"And what about you?" Marsala said, turning what Kerry was now sure was his mad gaze on her.

"I'm very sorry I helped you," Kerry admitted, which she knew wasn't a smart thing to say, but she couldn't help it.

The worst part was, she didn't think that had anything to do with what he said next: "How shall I kill you? I wish I knew if there was a way to reverse the vampire process."

"She's not a vampire," Ethan said, his first words since this had all begun.

Marsala held up his hands helplessly as though he hadn't even heard. "But who is there to ask whose answer I would trust?"

"*She's not a vampire,*" Ethan repeated more emphatically.

198

"Either someone's a vampire or not. There isn't any transitional stage—"

"Obviously the sunlight doesn't affect you," Marsala continued to Kerry. "And in any case, I'd offer you an easier death since this condition isn't your fault."

"SHE'S NOT A VAMPIRE!" Ethan yelled at him.

"You just let yourself get seduced by evil," Marsala said. "Just like Joey did. I wish there had been someone around to offer him an easy death." Marsala picked up one of the stakes and the mallet.

Kerry, keeping her back against the hallway wall, slid away in the direction of the bedrooms.

Marsala came after her.

Behind him, Ethan tried to get to his feet, but his right leg buckled under him.

Marsala whirled around, dropping the mallet as he reached for the gun in his belt.

"No!" Kerry screamed as he shot Ethan yet again in the leg.

Ethan dropped heavily to the floor.

She came running up behind Marsala, with no other plan than to make him stop hurting Ethan.

Marsala turned, and she found herself facing the gun in his right hand and the pointy stake in his left. Furious, she shoved him away from her.

She heard the gun go off yet again. She was sure she'd been hit—how could he have missed at such a distance?— but so far nothing hurt, and he was tipping over backward: He had flung his arms wide for balance, and the first thing she thought was that he had missed after all. And the second thing she thought was that he'd walked backward into his toolbox. And after that there was no time for thought as he fell down the stairs, hitting his head at least three different times before the final crack on the slate floor of the entryway.

It was no use going to check for a pulse. Kerry wasn't that familiar with dead people—Ethan and Regina excepted—but she knew Marsala was dead.

My fault, she thought. Though she'd only intended to push him away from her, she *had* pushed him, not realizing how close to the stairs they were. She spared a thought to think that she was sorry she'd killed him, but she couldn't be sorry he was dead. She spared another thought to think that she was glad she was alive, and then she was scrambling in the kitchen to drag the drape in front of the sliding-glass door.

"Kerry," Ethan called.

The sky was turning pink. It had to be a matter of seconds now.

She pulled the drape shut and headed for the living-room windows.

Ethan clutched her ankle as she passed, making her stumble and fall to her knees.

"What are you doing?" she screamed at him.

"The drapes aren't thick enough."

"Just let me . . ." She tried to wriggle free, but she could see that the drapes were an open weave, almost lace, all of them, and at the most they'd soften the sunlight. She could see the marks of fading on the carpet and furniture.

"Get the gun," Ethan told her.

She started to ask why, but she knew.

"I can't," she whispered.

Ethan released her ankle. "Kerry, I got caught by the dawn once before. It was only for a second, before I could bar the window." He looked at her desperately. "Please," he whispered, "a bullet through the brain will be much faster and less painful."

The gun had fallen out of Marsala's hand halfway down the stairs, so she didn't have to go all the way down, didn't have to look at the body of the man she had killed. She stood there, considering going the rest of the way down, considering going out, closing the door behind her, leaving nature to take its course without demanding any more of her. She probably wouldn't even be able to hear Ethan's screams as he began to die. Kerry picked the gun up, and it felt even colder and heavier than it had in the Student Union.

"Kerry," he called, which meant, *Hurry.*

She came back up to the top of the stairs, where she knelt because her legs couldn't carry her any farther. Her hand shook so that she had to hold the gun in both hands, and even then she thought she was going to miss entirely, or just inflict more damage, more pain, without killing him.

"It's all right," he assured her, closing his eyes, bracing himself.

But she hesitated, and he took in his next breath in a hiss of pain.

"Kerry!" he cried, a plea for her to be merciful. Then, as the soft glow of sunlight touched him: "God!"

She threw the gun into the kitchen. She was on her feet before it stopped skittering across the linoleum floor.

He'd flung his arms up, instinct to protect his face from the scorching rays of the sun.

Grabbing his wrists, she dragged him across the rug. She wasn't strong enough—she knew she wasn't; she'd get him only so far and then he'd die agonizingly—but she got him down the hall to the master bedroom and—mistrusting the looks of those drapes, too—into the closet. She pulled the doors shut, enclosing them in a space about five feet long and three wide.

But it was blissfully without sunlight.

She groped for the string she'd glimpsed, and the light came on.

Ethan was hunched over, breathing hard and ragged. Could vampires go into shock? she wondered.

She yanked one of Marsala's shirts off its hanger to use as a bandage around his leg.

"Not necessary," Ethan whispered, and—in fact—she saw that he was no longer bleeding.

She sat down, sliding her back down the wall, afraid of hitting the door and accidentally opening it on to the killing sunlight. "Lean against me," she told him.

He looked up at her with eyes made wide by pain and possibly mistrust, but he leaned against her—there was nothing else he could do.

She could feel the beating of his heart, brought to an almost human rate by fear and exertion.

"Don't be afraid," she said, though he had no reason to trust her. "I'll guard your sleep."

He closed his eyes.

He took one more breath . . .

. . . which he didn't exhale.

CHAPTER NINETEEN

EVENTUALLY MARSALA'S *Madame Butterfly* tape ended. Kerry could hear the sounds of traffic, very faintly, from outside. What if the police came to question Marsala again? What if a neighbor came to complain about all the noise in the earliest hours of the morning? Kerry was determined that she would protect Ethan, even if she had to hold the door closed with her fingernails against prying intruders.

Her arm became numb from his never-stirring position and she shifted him as gently as she could, even knowing that in all probability she *couldn't* wake him up, even if she wanted.

She began to think of how hungry she was, which made her think of how hungry he was likely to be, come rousing at sunset, which made her think that the most sensible thing to do was to kick open the closet door.

Anyone he kills after this, she thought, *it'll be like I killed them.* It was an unsettling thought.

But still she couldn't open the door.

Eventually she fell asleep, and when she did, she had another vampire dream.

It started, like the previous one, with Ethan's story of Regina making him into a vampire, except this time it was Kerry herself who lay by the side of the road, and when she looked up at the sound of footsteps approaching on the gravel, it was Ethan who stood there.

She looked up at him, afraid and expectant at the same time, and he knelt beside her, then sat, putting her head on his lap. She had lost so much blood from her vague and unspecified wounds that for once she felt cold and his touch was warm. Warm and gentle and sensuous, although all he touched was her face.

He leaned over her. "I won't hurt you," he whispered, so softly she couldn't make out the words, but she knew them by feeling the breath of them on her throat.

And then he bit her.

There was a moment of pain but, as he had promised, it felt very, very good. She was aware of her heart slowing as her life's blood drained out of her, and of his heart beating faster as her blood filled his veins; but still hers was faster than his.

Finally—she tried to pull him back—he straightened. Then he lifted his own wrist to his mouth and ran it across his teeth. Blood welled up, as it had done in the laundry when she'd accidentally cut him with the razor blade. *His and mine together this time,* she thought as it ran over the white cuff of his shirt and dripped onto the ground. He held his arm out to her. *"Choices,"* she remembered him saying, as he put his wrist to her mouth. At first she recoiled from the taste, but it filled her mouth and she had to spit it out or swallow. She swallowed. And a second time: she hesitated and the warm, coppery blood filled her mouth again. But then she began sucking on his wrist, drawing the blood from his arteries, unable to stop. He had his eyes closed, his head thrown back. She could feel his emotions running through her veins, sense his very thoughts as though they were her own. There were no more lies possible. There were no lies necessary.

She tugged on his arm till he was lying down with her, holding her against him so that she felt their hearts at last—at long last—beating in unison. He bit her neck again and began to drink back the blood she had just taken. Kerry realized there had to be more to it than this, that they couldn't survive forever on just each other's blood, but—*What the heck,* she thought, *it's just a dream; it doesn't have to make sense.*

But with that thought she woke up.

Ethan, of course, hadn't moved. Kerry, however, figured she'd better.

She stood, leaning him against the side wall, but the closet wasn't big enough for her to get as far away as she wanted. She glanced at her watch. Another two hours till sunset. Surely he'd be all right for two hours. But she didn't dare leave him, didn't dare open the door a crack for fear of the trickle of sunlight that would kill him.

Miserably, she sat back down on the floor at the greatest distance she could in this cramped space, a distance that was still so close she could touch him if she wanted, and she tried to convince herself she didn't want to.

Choices, she thought again. She had to make her own, and

205

those were the only ones she was responsible for. Not his. Not—this was a new thought—her mother's. *Let go of those,* she told herself.

It was the first time since her mother left that she felt free.

ETHAN GROANED AT 4:35 and woke with a shuddering breath.

"Welcome back," Kerry said.

Ethan looked at her warily. His hair had grown longer yet during the day's sleep, so that it hung loose in the ponytail holder she'd loaned him, giving him a rumpled look that his motionless sleep wouldn't have. He brushed the hair away from his face with the back of his hand. "I assumed you'd change your mind," he said softly.

"I told you I would watch over you." She didn't say that she had thought about it, but she imagined he probably knew that.

He sat up from his undignified slump, awkwardly, wincing with pain, as she pushed open the closet door. His face, especially on his cheeks below his eyes, was sunburned. When his shirt gaped at his neck, she could see that he was burned even where his clothes had covered his skin; he looked sunburned, like someone who had sat outside too long on the first sunny day of summer.

His arms, exposed where his sleeves had been rolled back, were blistered and raw.

"Will you recover?" she asked.

He nodded, grimacing as he evaluated the damage. "Much slower than from any other kind of injury," he said. "Slower even than it would take a human to heal . . . but eventually." He still hadn't gotten over his surprise at being alive, she could tell. "Thank you," he said.

206

She nodded. "I'm going home now," she told him. "I owed you this one day's protection, but my father doesn't even know yet whether I'm alive."

He got to his feet seconds after she did, slowed down by his injuries. "Kerry." He took her hands lightly in his own. He was warm, finally, the effect of the burns.

Which was too much like her dream.

"Why didn't you tell me they were all right?" she demanded, pulling her anger back up around her. "You knew how frantic I was. You *knew*."

"I also knew you wouldn't help me unless you thought your family was still in danger," he admitted.

What could she answer, when he was right? "Couldn't you think how crazy it'd make me to see it there in the paper and realize you'd known and hidden it from me?"

"He had a newspaper." Ethan groaned, finally putting things together. He shook his head. "I overlooked that possibility. I assumed Marsala would tell you, and that you'd think he was lying. I never stopped to think what would happen if he had proof."

She looked up into his eyes and tried not to let herself be distracted because he was so very attractive. Not: *I was wrong to lie,* but: *I was wrong to get caught.* "How would you have felt if our positions had been reversed?" she demanded. "If it was someone you loved? If I knew Regina was safe when you thought she was dead—"

"First of all," Ethan interrupted, reaching to touch her hair, "I already told you, Regina and I were not lovers—"

"No," Kerry interrupted him, "*first of all,* that is not the point. Second of all"—she punched his arm as hard as she could. He looked surprised, but didn't protest—"can't you say two sentences without lying? Every single time Regina's name comes up, you get all crazy, and you have the nerve to tell me you weren't lovers?" She turned her back on him and shrugged off the hand he put on her shoulder. "And third of all, I don't care if you were lovers or not."

"Kerry," Ethan said.

She refused to turn around.

"We were both vampires, sharing for a time the same small town. We were temporary companions of the night. Never lovers in any sense of the word. But I thought I'd led them to her. I thought I'd done something, and they'd found me out, and followed me, and killed her because of me. I thought it was my fault."

The idea that he, too, had been blaming himself for someone else's actions caused Kerry to turn around, and she made the mistake of looking into his eyes. She let him draw her in closer, let him kiss her—finally—on the lips. She put her arms around him, gently, so as not to hurt him, and for a few sweet moments let herself pretend that it could stay this way forever.

Which was a dangerous thought, considering.

"Ethan," she asked, remembering how he had made her fall asleep the night they had fled together so that she couldn't see how to get into the Rochester subway system, "can vampires affect people's dreams?"

"No," he said. He'd lied so often, about so many things, there was no reason to believe him now, except that she very much wanted to. And he did, she thought, sound puzzled by her question.

She could feel the strong but incredibly slow beating of his heart and knew that her own was going faster than it should have. He ran his hands over her back and shoulders, and she truly, truly didn't want to stop.

His kisses went lower, to her throat, which felt incredibly good. *I just want to know what it feels like,* she thought. *I'll stop him before it goes too far.* But then she thought that it had already gone too far. That it was already going to be the most difficult thing she had ever done to say—

"Ethan."

He kissed her lips again, perhaps to prevent her from speaking anymore.

She returned that kiss, then tipped her face away.

He resumed kissing her neck.

"Ethan."

He didn't stop, so she spoke even as he kissed her.

"Ethan, I just want you to know—not that anybody can ever *truly* know exactly how they're going to react to any given situation until they've actually been in that situation, and then it's too late because then you're saying how you *did* react instead of how you're *going to* react, so you can only guess. Which is what I'm doing, even though I don't have all the information, so you might think I'm being terribly naïve, which I probably am. But I don't want you thinking I'm implying any sort of criticism of anybody who may or may not have been in the same situation, which is obviously impossible anyway because every situation is different. . . ."

He had pulled back and was frowning, probably from concentration as he tried to follow what she was saying, and she couldn't fault him because she'd lost track herself.

Taking a deep breath, she said, "I just want to let you know that I don't intend to become a vampire."

He was studying her face, his blue eyes wide, but she couldn't tell what he was thinking, and it occurred to her that perhaps he had never intended to make her a vampire, that perhaps he was just going to get rid of the last witness in as kind and gentle a way as he could.

"In case the question ever comes up," she finished lamely.

He *was* startled, for he said, "Then why did you help me?"

"Because . . ." She looked away so he wouldn't see her eyes, which were suddenly filled with tears. "Because—stupid as it is—I love you."

He caressed her face and she threw her arms around him once again, sobbing into his chest before she remembered his burns and that she was probably hurting him. She pulled away and he leaned to kiss her, and she repeated, frantically, forcefully, "I don't intend to become a vampire."

She braced herself for the bite.

He hugged her, but without the intensity of before, and he rested his chin on her head as he rocked her slightly, more a comforting movement than anything else.

I could still change my mind, she thought, both wanting to and not.

And, because it was the last thing she wanted to do, she pulled away from him.

"If you aren't going to kill me," she said, "I need to know what to tell the police. What do I claim happened?"

Ethan studied her face. Then he sighed, looking away.

Kerry stared at the toes of her sneakers.

"Your father didn't come to pick you up," he said softly, calmly, with years and years' worth of experience, "so you accepted a ride home from Ethan Bryne, a customer at the store whom you'd chatted with before."

"Did I like him?" Kerry asked.

Ethan smiled. "Not all that much, but you were desperate for a ride."

"I don't think I like this story."

"It gets worse," Ethan assured her. "As the two of you walked out to his car, a man you did not then recognize, but who will turn out to be Gilbert Marsala, came out of the shadows. He had a gun and threatened to shoot unless Ethan drove where he was instructed, which turned out to be here, Marsala's home. Marsala put you in the sauna room in the basement, moving something heavy in front of the door so that you couldn't get out. You yelled for help, but apparently nobody heard you. After a long time—you had the impression it was the next night—Marsala came to get you out. You demanded to know what had happened to poor Ethan Bryne, but all Marsala would talk about was Satan and vampires."

"In favor or against?" Kerry interrupted.

"In favor of Satan but not vampires." Ethan stooped to touch a singed area on the rug where he had bled last night and where the sun had burned through.

She crouched across from him.

"I'll pour lighter fluid on these," he said, "and burn them even more. You can say Marsala raved about burning out all the vampire blood, including yours, which is when you shoved him, and he fell down the stairs. You were sure he was hurt but didn't realize he was dead; you just figured he'd be more furious than ever. You were sure that if you tried to go down those stairs, he'd grab you. You ran into the library and jammed the desk chair under the doorknob, certain he'd come banging on it any moment. You waited and waited. Eventually, you fell asleep. Finally, when you couldn't stand it anymore, you pulled the chair away and peeked down the stairs. It was only when you saw him in the same position that you realized he'd been dead all along. Unfortunately, because of your ordeal, you weren't thinking straight, so instead of calling the police from here, you walked home. Which will give me time to . . . arrange things here."

"What about Ethan Bryne?"

"Never to be seen again, I'm afraid."

"Are you really going to let me go?" she asked.

Ethan, still crouched by the burned bloodstain, held his hands up to indicate he wasn't going to stop her. "How can you ask that?" he said with what sounded like sincere hurt and amazement.

Which still might have meant either yes or no.

She made it to the door of the room before he stopped her.

He called, "Is there any chance you'd ever change your mind?"

She turned back. It was tempting. Faced with the prospect of never seeing him again, it was very tempting. But her only hope was not to let him see that. "Is there any chance you'd change yours?" she countered.

"It would be nice not to have to be looking over my shoulder all the time," he acknowledged. "And to see your hair in the sunlight." He glanced away as though embarrassed at the sentimentality of that. He made no assurances, which might have been more promising than if he did. "Good-bye, Kerry. In the future, be careful whom you rescue."

"Good-bye, Ethan," she said.

"Michel," he corrected, and because he gave it the French pronunciation, she thought maybe it was his real name.

It was more encouraging than any of his *honestlys* or *trulys*.

"Good-bye, Michel," she said. She walked down the stairs, past Marsala's body, and out the door, heading for home.